THE CHIMNEY SWEEP CHARM

MARCIA LYNN McCLURE

Published by Distractions Ink
P.O. Box 15971
Rio Rancho, NM 87174

Published by Distractions Ink
©Copyright 2011 by M. Meyers
A.K.A. Marcia Lynn McClure
Cover Photography by
©Francesco Cura and ©Mihai-bogdan Lazar | Dreamstime.com
Cover Design by
Sheri L. Brady | MightyPhoenixDesignStudio.com

1st Printed Edition: December 2011

McClure, Marcia Lynn, 1965—
The Chimney Sweep Charm: a novella/by Marcia Lynn McClure.

ISBN: 978-0-9852740-1-6

Library of Congress Control Number: 2011943676

Printed in the United States of America

To all of us who love…

Dick Van Dyke and Charles Dickens,
"Carol of the Bells" and peppermint-scented candles,
ragdolls and military veterans,
chestnuts roasting on an open fire,
and fluffy white muffs with chubby little children's hands
tucked warmly inside.
And, most of all, to all of us who simply love to bathe in all the
glories of Christmastime!

CHAPTER ONE

"Okay. Let's get started," the tall, gray-haired man standing at the front of the room began.

"I don't like orientations," Baylee Cabot whispered aside to the friend sitting next to her. "They always make me nervous for some reason."

Baylee's friend Candice giggled. "They make you nervous? Why?"

"I think I'm always afraid they'll throw something unexpected at me," Baylee explained.

"Like what?" Candice asked quietly. "We already have our costumes and schedules. What could they possible throw at us now?"

Baylee shrugged. "I don't know."

"What?" Candice asked. "Do you think they're going to announce that there's a bathing suit competition or something?"

Baylee frowned. "Of course not."

"Then quit worrying and listen up. Maybe we'll get free hot cocoa whenever we want or something like that."

1

"Though I would like to see you two in a bathing suit competition," Tate Polanski said as he turned around and winked at Baylee and Candice.

"Shut up, Tate," Baylee groaned, rolling her eyes. Tate drove her nuts. Actually, Tate drove everyone nuts. Oh sure, he was a great vocalist and supreme handbell ringer, but he was a pain in the neck too. In fact, at that moment Tate Polanski was the only negative thing Baylee could think of when it came to being a member of the Hampton Handbell Ringers.

"At this point, everyone should have their schedules," the tall, gray-haired man said. "If you don't have your schedules, see me immediately following the orientation."

Baylee sighed and focused her attention on the man addressing the room full of people. His name was John O'Sullivan, the events coordinator for the Dickens Village theme square.

"I'd like to begin our meeting by offering a little background into the Dickens Village, for those who might not be familiar with it," Mr. O'Sullivan said.

Baylee sighed again and settled back in her chair. Working evenings at the Dickens Village would be hard, but she was very excited to be doing so. Not only would the extra moonlighting with her handbell ringing group leave her with some great cash, but it would be fun to linger in the atmosphere and ambiance the Dickens Village offered.

"The Dickens Village is the brainchild of a man named Malcolm McBride," Mr. O'Sullivan said.

"Malcolm conceived the idea in the late 1970s, but it took him nearly thirty years to round up the investors, architects, and so forth needed to finance and construct such an undertaking as an entire recreation of an early 1800s English village here in the US. Still, Malcolm managed it somehow, and in the year 2000 construction began on the Dickens Village—a theme commons meant to transport visitors back to the time of Charles Dickens."

Baylee smiled. Oh, she already knew the history of the Dickens Village—but she loved hearing it all the same. She listened with interest as Mr. O'Sullivan began to read from a pamphlet he'd taken out of his pocket.

"The Dickens Village is composed of several square blocks of buildings that comprise retail establishments and dwellings, fashioned to emulate Camden Town in London, England, the way it may have appeared in 1843…the year Charles Dickens's *A Christmas Carol* was first published." Mr. O'Sullivan paused, looking out over the gathered conglomeration of retail workers, vendors, and security personnel that had congregated for the orientation. "I'm assuming all of you have visited the Dickens Village at one time or another." There was a general hum of yeses and nodding heads. "Then you know how truly magical a place it is." Again hums of yeses and other agreeing sounds. "Good," Mr. O'Sullivan continued, "because by accepting holiday employment or vending space with the Dickens Village, you have agreed to take on the responsibility of ensuring that each and every visitor this holiday season enjoys themselves to the fullest."

Baylee liked the warm, delighted sensation that was welling in her chest. She loved the Dickens Village—she always had. And to have the opportunity to perform with the Hampton Handbell Ringers and Carolers in the Dickens Village for two entire months during the holidays would be a dream come true! Baylee brushed a stray strand of caramel-highlighted brown hair from her cheek, thinking of how grateful she was she'd managed to pass the five auditions necessary to make it into the Hampton Handbell Ringers the year before. Sure, it was a lot of work—a ton of practicing was necessary—but whenever she was performing with the others, whether in public or just in practice, every one of Baylee's five senses was overjoyed.

Handbell ringing was a vanishing and somewhat magical novelty. Yet Baylee had loved the beautiful chimes of a handbell choir since the moment she'd first heard one at the age of three. She'd never forget it. She'd been watching television—something her mother was watching on PBS—and a handbell choir had performed "Carol of the Bells." Baylee had never heard anything so beautiful—not in all her long three years upon the earth! She'd been mesmerized by handbells ever since and had begun begging for her own set handbells the very next Christmas.

Though her parents had complied, gifting her a new handbell each year as one of her Christmas presents, it wasn't until she was in the sixth grade that

Baylee had really begun to learn the skill and art of handbell ringing. When she had been able to finally audition for a local handbell choir in middle school, her love of handbells and handbell ringing had really begun to know a measure of satisfaction. She'd continued with the same handbell choir through high school, eventually leaving it for the opportunity to join the Randolph Handbell Ringers. It was while ringing with Randolph's that Baylee discovered she owned a pretty darn good soprano singing voice as well. In fact, during her first interview with the Hampton Handbell Ringers, the conductor had asked her why it was she hadn't been singing all her life—why it had taken her until she started college to earn her music degree to realize it. Baylee simply explained that she'd always focused on the music of the bells she'd heard in her head and had never really noticed she could sing until college.

And now, as she sat listening to Mr. O'Sullivan describe the new vendors and shops that had been added to the Dickens Village for the holidays, Baylee thought there could be no more beautiful thing on earth than to be dressed in Dickens's era clothing and wandering the cobblestone streets ringing or singing Christmas carols to all the world.

"We're really excited about having the Hampton Handbell Ringers and Carolers aboard for this season," Mr. O'Sullivan said. He smiled at the group of bell ringers sitting on the first two rows. "I've heard you all perform so many times, and as glorious as it was...I can't imagine how truly amazing it's going to be to see you roaming the streets of the Dickens Village this year."

Baylee smiled, thinking that Mr. O'Sullivan must indeed be a like-minded soul to her. She could tell he truly appreciated the beauty of handbells—and not just because of the price he'd agreed to pay the Hampton Handbell Ringers and Carolers to perform at the Dickens Village.

"He hasn't said anything about a bathing suit competition yet," Candice whispered.

"Thank goodness," Baylee quietly giggled.

"There's another new addition to this year's holiday festivities," Mr. O'Sullivan said. "And that's a larger security force than we've had before."

Baylee frowned a little. She didn't like to think of that fact that the Dickens Village needed security—though she knew it did. It seemed every inch of everywhere needed security any more.

She was a little relieved when Mr. Sullivan explained, "Of course, the visitors won't know they're there. Our security team will be incognito, as always."

Baylee was glad to know that at least it wouldn't look like the streets of old Camden Town at Christmas were operating under martial law.

"But we do want all of you to know who you can contact if you see anything amiss or have trouble yourself," Mr. O'Sullivan said. Nodding toward someone in the audience, he asked, "Brian? Would you like to give us a little update on exactly who we can to

6

contact if the need should arise? For those of you who might not already know him, Brian is our new head of security."

"You bet," a man sitting about halfway back in the middle of the room said.

Baylee watched the man as he stood up, trying to memorize his face in case she ever needed the assistance of the security staff—though she couldn't imagine why she ever would. The head of security, Brian, was in truth a very handsome guy. He was the archetypal tall, dark, and handsome hero type—with brown eyes, black hair, and biceps the size of tree trunks.

"All of a sudden, I'm a little more excited about this particular bell-ringing gig," Candice whispered to Baylee as she too studied Brian, the head of security.

"Absolutely," Baylee agreed.

"I'm Brian Reagan, and my security teams are the best available," the handsome head of security began. "As John said, we're bringing in some extra guys for the holidays...so you'll be surrounded by multiple safety measures."

"Hmmm," Candice mumbled. "I'd be fine if it were just *him* who was surrounding me."

"Absolutely," Baylee giggled.

"If you need help," Brian continued, "just let one of us know. We will be positioned throughout the village and dressed up like all of you, of course. For example, the roasted chestnut vendor, the hot soup vendor, and an older guy who might look a lot to you like Ebenezer Scrooge—" He paused to allow for everyone's laughter to die down and then continued, "They'll be right in the center of town, near the fountain. Beyond that, all you need to do is find yourself a chimney sweep, and you've got one of us on the line. We figured chimney sweeps, with their smudged-up faces and black-ops uniforms, would be the stealth way to keep watch. With the chimney sweep thing, we can be wherever we want to without looking out of place—rooftops, streets, shops, dwellings…everywhere. So if you need something, just grab a chimney sweep."

"Well, there you go," Baylee whispered to Candice. "That's easy enough to remember. If we need help, we just look for Dick Van Dyke and sing 'Chim Chim Cher-ee.'"

"I'm totally down with that," Candice whispered in return. "I *love* Dick Van Dyke!"

"Me too," Baylee said quietly. "I always thought Mary Poppins was an idiot for not giving up the nanny gig to go for Bert."

"Worst mistake of her life," Candice agreed in a mumble.

"I'll have the guys stand up so you can see how many of us there are," Brian said. "And remember, half the staff is already on duty over at the village. Guys?"

There was the muffled sound of audience members standing up, and Baylee and Candice turned to look behind them.

"Holy smokes!" Baylee breathed.

"It's like a Navy SEAL convention or something," Candice added.

And it was! Baylee couldn't believe that over twenty-five of the people in the orientation audience were tall, dark, handsome, buff guys dressed all in black. Each man stood with his feet apart and hands held at his back—similar if not exactly like a military "at ease" stance.

"They're all packing heat too," Baylee whispered to Candice as she noted all the holstered sidearms.

"I guess Mr. O'Sullivan wants to be prepared," Candice said.

"I suppose you girls are all wowed now, right?" Tate said from the front row.

"Let's see," Candice began, looking to Tate and feigning an expression of thoughtfulness. "Let's say I'm being assaulted by some weirdo in the street... and who am I going to look to for protection? One of these guys?" she said, nodding toward the security staff. "Or you, Tate? You...who freaked out in June when we were in New York and you thought some guy was looking at you funny. You freaked out and slammed Megan's finger in the door and cut it off! Who do you think I'm going to trust?"

"It was an accident, and you know it," Tate grumbled.

Baylee did know it. Still, she found her eyes glancing down the row of chairs in front of her to Megan—to the missing first joint and fingertip on her right hand.

"Yeah, it was," Candice admitted. "But you still cared more about yourself than Megan. The guy was stalking Megan...not you. Real heroic, Tate. Way to go to instilling a sense of confidence in me that you would have my back."

"Whatever," Tate grumbled, turning around in his seat to pout.

"Thank you," Brian said to his men. Baylee watched as the security staff sat down in unison. "So there you have it…our extra security staff for the next two months. As I said, if you need assistance…just grab a chimney sweep."

Baylee giggled. "Grab a cab, grab a snack…grab a chimney sweep."

Candice giggled too. "And you know what? I just figured out what I want for Christmas."

"Absolutely," Baylee agreed. "I'll never ring 'Chim Chim Cher-ee' with the same mental pictures again."

They giggled together, biting their lips and binding their tongues when Mr. O'Sullivan's attention lingered rather scoldingly on them a moment.

Baylee knew their joking around might sound scandalous to anyone listening, but they were only kidding. Sure, the security guys were attractive—a striking group of militant-looking hero-types—but in truth they were probably a bunch of egotistical gun freaks. She wondered how they felt about being dressed up as chimney sweeps and skulking around in a reproduction of an old London town, which was no doubt already slathered in Christmas decor.

"Thank you, Brian," Mr. O'Sullivan said. "Next I'd like to make you all aware of some new vendors we have for this year's holiday season."

Baylee smiled, amused by their ridiculous comments concerning the security staff guys. Yet as she tried to focus once more on what Mr. O'Sullivan was saying—on the new ragdoll vendor he'd just introduced—a strange sensation began to travel up the back of her neck. It wasn't an unpleasant sensation at all—just strange. She felt as if an old electric heating pad had been pressed to the back of her neck—had the odd feeling that someone sitting behind her was significant to her somehow.

But she brushed the sensation aside. After all, twenty-five intimidating Navy SEAL types were sitting behind her, armed to the teeth. Who wouldn't feel weird?

❦

"Well, I guess tomorrow night will find us dressed up like the Cratchit kids and ringing our little hearts out," Candice said as Baylee walked with her across the parking lot toward their cars. The parking lot of the Dickens Village office headquarters was quickly emptying, but Baylee was in no hurry. She and Candice had discovered that one of the opinions they shared was that *not* racing to get out of a parking lot was far wiser, as well as safer, than rushing into a fender bender, or worse. Yep, they'd each discovered that the spring before when hurrying to meet some friends for dinner after handbell practice one night—and had found Candice's car T-boned and Candice in the hospital for three days.

And so, as others associated with the Dickens

Village orientation hurried on, Baylee and Candice contentedly meandered toward their cars.

"Wanna know a secret?" Baylee asked her friend.

"Always," Candice answered.

"Do you think it's weird that I'm so excited about this? I mean, I can't wait to get there tomorrow night... to see people's faces when they hear the bells."

"I don't think you're weird at all," Candice said. "I know how you feel about the bells. There's something vintage about handbells. That's why we love them so much. That's why we do what we do. The bells are, like, totally magical. They make people feel things they don't feel very often anymore." Baylee nodded. "We've got the rest of our lives to teach music or whatever...but we might not always be able to have handbell ringing as our career."

"That's true," Baylee agreed. "Think of all the emotions you can see washing over people's faces when we perform. Things like true, tingly joy," Baylee suggested.

"And the sensation of a sincere smile," Candice added.

"And, of course, the most important emotion..." Baylee began.

Giggling, both girls sighed, "Love!"

"And there they are...the two little goody-goody girls."

At the sound of Tate's voice behind them, Baylee's heart sank to the pit of her stomach. Something about Tate Polanski just made her skin crawl. Though she'd never said a word about it out loud, she secretly hoped that Mr. Hampton would get fed up with Tate's irritating personality and drop-kick him out of the Hampton Handbell Ringers. But since it was a terrible thing to think toward someone, Baylee always just bit her tongue—even when Candice would rant her own disgust concerning Tate.

"Good-bye, Tate," Candice said as Tate stepped between her and Baylee. "We don't have time for your crap today."

"But wait," Tate said, taking hold of Baylee's arm with one hand and Candice's with the other and pulling them to a halt. "Don't you want to hear what I just found out about those beefy security guys you two were drooling over at the orientation meeting?"

"We were not drooling over them, Tate," Baylee countered.

"I was," Candice playfully interjected.

"Yes, you were, Candice…and so were you, Baylee," Tate mocked. "Anyway, I thought you two might just want to know where these guys came from before you go off trying to reel a couple of them into your boyfriend traps."

"I really don't care, Tate," Baylee said. "And let go of my arm." She tried to pull her arm free, but Tate held tight.

"All those black-clad, muscle-bound, jarheads types in there," he continued however. "That's exactly what they are—jarheads."

"What are you talking about?" Candice asked,

the irritation growing in her voice as she too tried to disengage her arm from Tate's grasp.

"They're jarheads. They're exactly what they look like," he answered.

"You mean they're Marines?" Baylee asked. "Like, ex-Marines?"

Tate shrugged. "Maybe not all of them are Marines, but they're all ex-military somethings...Army, Marines, Navy...whatever. They're all ex-military."

"Well, good," Baylee said, wrenching her arm free at last. "I feel safer already." She glared at Tate. Oooo! He drove her nuts!

"Do you?" he asked, however, taking hold of her arm again. "You feel safer having a bunch of ex-military, discharged for medical reasons, chimney sweeps hopping over rooftops at the Dickens Village? I'm telling you, some of these guys are literally insane."

"And how do you know that?" Candice asked.

"I overheard Mr. O'Sullivan talking to buffed-up head of security," he explained. "Some of these guys were wounded in action, some of them just didn't reenlist when their time was up, and some of them were discharged for psychological reasons...and that makes you feel more safe?"

"Absolutely," Baylee said through gritted teeth.

Tate frowned at her a moment. "Who are you? Rocky Balboa or something?"

"Ex-military," Candice said. "Seems to me they'd make the best security force."

But Tate growled with disgust, shaking his head.

"They're ex-soldiers, ladies. Damaged goods. It ain't like it's gonna be Dick Van Dyke leaping around on those rooftops while we're performing. It'll be jarheads and nut jobs."

"For your information, Tate," Baylee began, attempting to keep her temper reined in. "Dick Van Dyke is a military veteran himself. He was in the United States Army Air Corps during World War II…which apparently you did not know. So keep your opinions to yourself. I'm glad they're all ex-military…whether or not they're dressed like chimney sweeps."

A knowing grin spread across Tate's face, and he only egged Baylee on by saying, "Oooo! Those pretty brown eyes of yours are blazing now, aren't they, Baylee Cabot? You really do have a thing for those jarheads, don't you?"

"Excuse me."

"Holy smokes!" she heard Candice breathe.

Baylee glanced up to see two members of the new security staff standing behind them—and they were both more than merely striking. Though one man was far and away more handsome than the other, they were both attractive—as well as intimidating.

One of the men nodded to Tate and asked, "You're one of the handbell ringers, right?"

"Yeah," Tate managed to answer.

"I heard you guys are really good," the more handsome one said.

Baylee stared at him for a moment—because he was certainly a sight to behold. He was tall, with an unusual

15

color of brown hair (that reminded her of Brazil nut shells), and green eyes that looked fabulous against his dark complexion.

"We've been told we're the best," Tate countered.

"Cool," the exceptionally good-looking chimney-sweep-to-be said. "I can't wait to see you guys do your thing."

"Me neither," the other agreed.

Baylee couldn't help but smile a little—for she knew exactly what the two security guys were doing. As the too-handsome-for-words guy stepped between her and Tate, gently disengaging Tate's hand from her arm, the other guy did the same thing as he stepped between Tate and Candice. They were intimidating Tate but under the guise of interest in the Hampton Handbell Ringers.

"Excuse me," the sinfully handsome guy said, still looking at Tate. "We've gotta get going. I guess we'll see you tomorrow night, right?"

"I guess so," Tate mumbled. He was mad—furious. And the expression of irritation on his face was fabulous!

"Ladies," the dazzlingly handsome guy said, looking quickly to Candice and then to Baylee.

"You all have a good evening," the other guy aded, nodding to Tate. And then they simply sauntered toward their vehicles.

"Well, that's nauseatingly predictable," Tate mumbled as Baylee watched each security guy climb into a pickup. The wickedly handsome guy was driving, and as the big black Dodge Ram drove away, Baylee noted the Silver Star license plate on the front bumper of the truck and the Purple Heart license plate on the back. Both were embellished with license plate frames that read *Iraq/Afganistan Veteran—US Army Ranger*.

"Wow!" Baylee heard herself whisper.

"Wow is right," Tate grumbled. "Egotistical jarheads."

But Baylee was the daughter of a Gulf War veteran—the granddaughter of a Vietnam veteran as well.

And as her irritation and disgust with Tate heightened, she turned to him and said, "You know what, Tate? You have no idea. What's the worst thing you've ever had to do? Have a cavity filled at the dentist's office? So shut up. The Silver Star?" she asked, pointing in the direction the two military veterans had driven off in. "The Purple Heart? That's wounded in combat…and the Silver Star is for valor in the face of the enemy. So go on and whine about the fact that these guys are working security for whatever reason. I'll tell you this—I'd rather have chimney sweeps with Purple Heart medals pinned to their chests keeping things in line wherever I'm working than to have to depend on you for anything! So shut up and go home!"

"Geez, Baylee," Tate whined. "Take a lozenge and calm down."

"And don't lay a hand on me again, okay?" she added, turning from him and storming off toward her car.

"I guess Tate didn't get the memo about your

feelings where the military is concerned," Candice laughed as she hurriedly caught up to Baylee.

Baylee shook her head. "Tate Polanski makes me sick," she growled. "It's guys like him...people like that...they're what's wrong with this country. They've never had to suffer or do without or live in fear of having their freedom stripped away. I just can't tolerate him anymore today. I swear, half the time I want to take his bells and shove them down his throat!"

"I love when you lose your cool," Candice giggled. "You so seldom do. But when you do...*bam*! I love it!"

"I don't," Baylee admitted, exhaling a heavy sigh.

"Well, don't let it bother you...and don't let Tate bother you. Think about those handsome ex-whatever-they-ares and the fact that they'll be working at the Dickens Village with us for two whole months." Candice giggled. "Did you see the way they just so smoothly interceded between us and Tate? Smooth and cool like nothing I've ever seen."

Baylee smiled again too. "Yeah. And that made it official."

"Made what official?" Candice asked.

"I officially know exactly what I want for Christmas," Baylee answered, smiling at her friend.

"A chimney sweep?" Candice asked knowingly.

"Absolutely!" Baylee confirmed.

"What an idiot," Justice Kincaid mumbled as he drove out of the Dickens Village office parking lot.

"*Freaking* idiot," his friend Tristan embellished. "Guys like that just chap my—"

"I know," Justice agreed. He grinned however, glanced to Tristan, and added, "But that one little bell ringer girl was shweet, right?"

"Both of them were," Tristan answered.

Justice sighed as he turned onto the main road. "Did you ever think we'd be pulling security duty at some theme park dressed like chimney sweeps, dude?"

"Hell no!" Tristan laughed. He shook his head. "But maybe this gig will be more interesting than we think. Especially if the intel is correct."

"Roger that," Justice chuckled.

He raked a hand over his short dark hair. "I just hope that handbell choir group thing doesn't play 'Chim Chim Cher-ee.' I might be overcome by the urge to start leaping around over rooftops like Dick Van Dyke."

"Who?" Tristan asked.

"Dude!" Justice exclaimed, frowning at his friend. "Are you kidding me? Dick Van Dyke? *Mary Poppins*?" But Tristan just shrugged with an expression of ignorance on the subject. Justice shook his head and mumbled, "Man…growing up without sisters really must've jacked you up. You don't even know who Dick Van Dyke is."

"Maybe not," Tristan admitted. "But I know who that idiot who was just handling those bell ringer girls is…and I plan to keep him in my sights. I hate dudes like that."

"Absolutely," Justice agreed. "Abso-freakin'-lutely."

Justice turned on the satellite radio, tuned it to the classic rock station, and heightened the volume. He was trying to distract himself from the weird sensation he'd had when he'd stepped between the guy bell ringer moron and the pretty girl he'd been man-handling. He hadn't even looked at the girl more than once—and he hadn't because of the strange wave of warmth that had washed over him in simply knowing she was there. It was kind of creepy—the way her image was lingering in his mind even at that very moment—like he already knew her or had seen her somewhere before. He didn't even know the shweet honey's name, but somehow he felt like he should.

He shook his head in an effort to dispel the vision of the girl from his mind. Yet he thought twice about it and decided to keep her there. After all, why chase away something so pretty and sweet, when there were so many other things clicking around in his brain that were exactly the opposite?

"Chimney sweeps, dude," Tristan chuckled. "I like it."

Justice nodded. "Me too," he said, still thinking about the cute bell ringer girl. "Me too."

CHAPTER TWO

"It's so pretty I'm gonna die!" Baylee exclaimed as she and Candice stepped through the ornate iron gates leading from the Dickens Village parking lot to the village itself. "I mean, look at that! Can you even believe it?"

Baylee was truly awestruck. In all her life she'd never seen anything like the Dickens Village as it stood all dressed up for the holidays.

"Haven't you been here before?" Candice asked.

"Well, yeah," Baylee answered, "but never when it was all lit up for Christmas like this! I only moved here in January, remember?" She shook her head in awed wonder. "I cannot believe this!"

Baylee was experiencing something nearly magical. For just a moment, she actually felt like she'd stepped out of the modern world and into a beautiful, warm-lighted globe created by Charles Dickens. In truth, she knew the London Camden Town of 1843 would've appeared much differently than the electric-lighted reproduction she was walking into now—but the sensation of having stepped into the past washed over with such command that, even for the warm red velvet caroler costume she was wearing, her entire body rippled with goose bumps.

Everywhere she looked she saw only beauty— pure loveliness! The buildings loomed dark against the evening sky, but every old-fashioned paned window was lit golden with flickering candlelight. Pine boughs strewn with red berries were draped overhead across the main streets. Christmas wreaths made of more pine boughs, holly sprigs, and pinecones hung on every door. Mistletoe balls, adorned with red ribbon, hung from every lamppost. The buildings and vendor carts seemed drenched in winter greenery and red berry sprigs. The cheering scent of burning pine was in the air—of cinnamon and freshly baked bread.

Baylee inhaled deeply. "Do you smell that? It actually smells as good as it looks!"

Candice giggled. "Girl, you need to get out more."

Baylee smiled and countered, "Girl, you need to appreciate things more."

"Look!" Candice suddenly exclaimed. Pointing to a nearby shop, she said, "There goes one now."

"One what?" Baylee asked, turning her attention to the shop Candice was indicating.

Candice rolled her eyes. "A chimney sweep, you goof."

Baylee saw him then—a man dressed all in black, with soot smudging his face. She smiled when she noted the authenticity of his costume. He seriously looked as if he'd just leapt out of a Dickens novel! He wore black pants and boots, a tattered, soot-dusted white shirt and black vest, a tight-fitting tailed jacket with silver buttons, fingerless gloves, and a ragged top hat. He even had a chimney sweep brush propped on one shoulder.

"I totally want one," Baylee giggled.

"I know!" Taking hold of Baylee's sleeve, Candice tugged her arm. "Come on. We have a few minutes before we're supposed to meet the others. Let's get a closer look at that that guy."

"Absolutely," Baylee readily agreed. After all, she was just as curious about the chimney sweep security staff as Candice was. She did doubt, however, that she'd find any member of the security staff interesting at all after having had a look at the exceptionally gorgeous one who had stepped between she and Tate the day before. Even in that moment, she couldn't believe how handsome he'd been—how her skin had instantly warmed at just the sight of him.

As Baylee and Candice hurried toward the shop into which the chimney sweep had disappeared, a young boy with a wooden crutch tucked under one arm hobbled toward them.

He was dressed in Dickens period costume, and as he approached, he lifted his hat, nodded to Baylee and Candice, and said, "God bless us, every one!"

Baylee smiled and asked, "You're Tiny Tim then?"

"Yes, milady," the boy answered. He smiled at her, studied her from head to toe a moment, and said,

"And you must be a couple of the handbell ringers Mr. O'Sullivan told us about today. Nice costumes."

"Thanks," Baylee said. She removed one of her hands from the white muff she'd had it tucked in and smoothed the red velvet of her dress.

"The matching cape is cool," the boy commented. "Do your shoes match too?"

"Well, they're not velvet, of course, but they match for the time period we're in," Baylee giggled. Hitching up the hem of her dress, she displayed the black Victorian lace-up boots she was wearing. The boy smiled.

"You guys look totally real. Good job," he complimented.

"How about this?" Baylee asked as she lifted the hood of her matching red velvet cape, trimmed in white fur, to cover the back of her neck and head. She tucked her hand back into the muff she held and asked, "Better?"

"Perfect!' the boy laughed. He looked to Candice and said, "Do all you guys match like this?"

"The guys were other stuff," Candice answered. "You know, top hats, black tailcoats…that kind of stuff."

"I can't wait to see them," the boy said. "My grandpa owns this place and let me be Tiny Tim some of the time this year." Removing his hat, he said, "Malcolm McBride the Third, ladies…in case you ever need to know."

Baylee smiled and nodded at the boy. "Thanks,

Malcolm. I'm Baylee, and this is Candice. You should come listen to our bells tonight if you can."

"Oh, I will for sure. Happy holidays!" he chimed as he hurried off.

Baylee and Candice watched him bolt away—laughed when the boy seemed to realize he was supposed to be a sickly Tiny Tim and began limping once more.

"Well, he's just too adorable for words," Candice said as she opened the door to the shop before them and stepped in.

A bell sounded as the door opened, and both Baylee and Candice gasped as their eyes beheld the dreamlike glory within the tiny shop. China dolls were everywhere! Nestled in among beautiful Victorian-era dollhouses, vintage-looking china dolls waited in small rocking chairs or in handcrafted cradles to be purchased.

"It's a doll shop," Baylee mumbled.

"You've got it, Sherlock," Candice teased.

Baylee playfully rammed an elbow into Candice's ribcage as she continued to look around the room. "I could spend hours in here," she sighed.

"Me too," Candice agreed. "Only we don't have hours...and it looks like the chimney sweep has already ducked out." Candice frowned and grumbled, "Dang it! How could he disappear so fast?"

"Well, I guess we'll just have to find another one later," Baylee said. "We've got to go. I don't want to be late and catch it from Mr. Hampton."

"Chimney sweeps and dolls will just have to wait," Candice sighed with disappointment.

As the girls hurried from the shop and toward the fountain in the center of town, Baylee knew it was going to be nearly impossible for her to concentrate on handbell ringing when the Dickens Village offered so much beauty and nostalgic atmosphere to bathe in. Still, she loved ringing and singing Christmas carols. Her time at the Dickens Village would be wonderful! She knew it would, and the joy swelling in her bosom warmed her to the very core of her heart.

❦

Justice rubbed at his eyes a moment. He should've gotten a better night's sleep. If he weren't at his best, he wouldn't do the team any good if or when the maniac they were looking for *did* decide to show up at the Dickens Village. He shook his head and exhaled a heavy sigh, knowing all too well that he would never be wholly at his best again—not after Afghanistan. Still, he was alive, and everything that had been broken, lacerated, or mashed had healed as well as it would. Changing the attitude of his train of thought, Justice reminded his sore shoulder how lucky it was to be in the shape it was in.

Inhaling a deep breath of the crisp, cool night air, he was surprised at how truly great it smelled. He could smell the bread baking in the bakery, already knowing he was near its chimney. It made his stomach growl with hunger—as the scent of freshly baked bread always did. His mouth began to water as the thought of warm bread slathered in butter flitted through his mind.

Gazing out over the little nostalgic village, Justice admitted that it was quite an amazing thing—a reproduction of mid-1800s Camden Town right there on the outskirts of the big city. Of course, he could look behind him and see the skyscrapers of the busy metropolises stretching up into the sky. But the visitors to the Dickens Village on the streets below him were completely unaware of them. He smiled, liking the fact that the people enjoying the shops and sight in the Dickens Village were able to escape their worries and fast-paced lives for a time. He just hoped his team could keep them all safe.

It was Justice's opinion that Malcolm McBride should've let John O'Sullivan in on the truth about the added security—that the FBI was on the trail of a notorious psychopath who believed he was the actual Jack the Ripper and that recent evidence implied that the Dickens Village might be his next focus in searching for victims. But Brian had agreed that only a few higher-ups would know about the operation.

And so, there he stood, perched on top of a reproduction Camden Town building, dressed as a chimney sweep. He smiled, chuckling with amusement as "Chim Chim Cher-ee" began echoing in his mind.

Justice's thoughts were suddenly scattered, however—by the most beautiful sound he could ever remember hearing. Stealthily altering his position, he looked down to see the handbell ringers gathered in the square and beginning to perform. As he recognized the opening of "Carol of the Bells," he held his breath a moment. "Carol of the Bells" was one of his favorite Christmas carols—and he knew how easily it could be butchered. It seemed most choirs or musicians either played it so fast that it felt like a horse race or so slow that it made him want to nod off.

Yet as the Hampton Handbell Ringers moved into the full cadence of the carol, Justice grinned. "Perfect," he whispered. And it was. He'd never heard anything like it—not in real life anyway. The perfect measure of the bells—the way their tinkling sounds rang out into the night—gave his heart a lift. For just an instant, he owned the same delight in knowing the holidays were at hand as he had when he was a little kid. The sensation only lasted an instant, but it was powerful—and welcomed.

Justice's grandmother had been a great fan of "Carol of the Bells" and had owned a set of chimes she played the song on each Christmas Eve. He wondered for a moment if she still owned the chimes—missed being a carefree child who believed in Santa Claus and that his parents could protect him from any and all harm in the world.

The impression of childlike joy was fleeting, but the beautiful ringing of the bells wasn't, and Justice stood mesmerized as he watched the handbell ringers perform—specifically the pretty little thing he'd attempted to champion the day before in the parking lot.

The young woman stood center front, holding a shiny brass handbell in each hand and playing each one in turn with the grace and countenance of any Christmas angel that ever sat atop any Christmas tree. She was dressed all in red velvet and white fur—of course, all the women were—but for some reason Justice thought her red velvet dress and hooded cape looked brighter than the others.

He focused on the girl for a long time—entirely fascinated by everything about her. And then, as "Carol of the Bells" ended, he was even more amazed when it began again—this time with the handbell ringers performing the carol vocally. The a cappella vocal rendition of the piece was nearly as stirring as the handbell rendition. And Justice smiled when he picked out the voice of his favorite handbell ringer—first soprano.

He sighed—awed at the peace and tranquility the handbell ringers caroling were sifting into the night. He felt in that moment that all *was* calm. He knew it wasn't, of course. He knew men, women, and children were lingering in misery in many places all over the world—that people were suffering with loss, desperation, pain, and agony. Yet something about the carolers—they'd soothed his soul for a time. He couldn't remember the last time he'd experienced a feeling of calm. Sure, it was brief—but it was wonderful.

Then, as his eyes darted to a man cloaked in black and wearing a tall top hat, he was all too aware of exactly why he was there on the rooftops of the Dickens Village.

But as the man bent down and picked up a small boy to put him on his shoulders—and being that the boy's face was radiating with love and recognition—he figured it was safe to listen to the carolers for a moment again. It was a lovely sound, and Justice wondered if the fact that he'd thought the word *lovely* meant he was getting too complacent.

Straightening his posture and refocusing his attention on why he was there, he pulled the small set of binoculars from his pocket and began studying the people gathered in the square.

"A Jack the Ripper copycat," he grumbled to himself. "What next?"

❦

"Oh, but look at this one!" Candice exclaimed. "You so need it! It looks so much like us!"

Baylee smiled as Candice handed her the small sterling silver charm fashioned to look like a Victorian caroler. "It does look like us," she said, studying the charm. "It really does. She even has a muff."

"You totally need that for your good bracelet," Candice said.

Baylee turned over the little box housing the charm to look at the price. "Ouch! It's thirty bucks," she whispered to Candice.

"Oh, come on," Candice pleaded, however. "I'll go halves with you. It's too perfect not to be dangling from your wrist."

Baylee giggled, for she wholeheartedly agreed with Candice. The Victorian caroler charm *was* perfect for her charm bracelet! "It is perfect...and you don't have to go halves with me. I'll buy it." Handing the pretty charm in the red velvet box to the lady behind the jewelry shop counter, Baylee nodded and said, "I just have to have it."

"It looks just like you," the lady said. "I can see why you can't pass it up." The woman moved to the cash register and scanned the price sticker barcode on the bottom of the box. "Cash, debit, or charge?"

"Cash," Baylee said, reaching into her red velvet dress pocket and retrieving the small change purse in which she carried her cash and ID when performing.

"It's so cute, Baylee!" Candice chimed again. "Really it is. It's just too perfect for you."

"I know," Baylee agreed. The sterling Victorian caroler charm would look so pretty on her new bracelet. She couldn't wait to attach it!

Ever since she'd been a little girl, Baylee Cabot had wanted a charm bracelet—not a little kids' one, but a real charm bracelet with real charms. Once she was old enough and had some spending money here and there, she'd begun making her own charm bracelets, and they were pretty ones too. However, she'd still wanted a real one—sterling silver or gold. Thus, when she'd landed the job with the Hampton Handbell Ringers and moved away from home, the first luxury she'd allowed herself was the purchase of a sterling silver charm bracelet.

Baylee soon discovered, however, that the sort of charms she liked were pretty pricey, and so she'd promised herself she'd only buy a charm when one appeared that she fell in love with—literally loved and knew she'd never find another one like it. She'd also promised herself that each charm she did purchase would need to be significant—have a memory or some sort of favoritism attached. And the moment she'd seen the Victorian caroler charm, she'd known both requirements to validate a charm purchase were fulfilled—even without Candice's encouragement she'd known it.

The Victorian caroler charm was not only beautiful but far and away singular because it was a Victorian caroler (just as Baylee and Candice were) but also because she had purchased it at the Dickens Village. It would be so lastingly meaningful—the fact that she'd purchased the charm right there at the jewelry shop in the Dickens Village.

As she handed the price of the charm to the jewelry shop clerk, Baylee sighed. It was such a lovely little bracelet charm!

"Thank you," the clerk said, handing Baylee a small brown paper bag stamped with holly and berries. "It really is a very beautiful charm…just like the music you girls are providing the village this year. I can't believe how beautiful those handbells are!"

"Thank you," Baylee said. "And I'm sure we'll be back to browse around. It's only our first day on the job, and already we've spent every penny we earned today."

"Oh, believe me…if anybody knows how hard it is

to work here and not spend money, it's me!" the woman laughed. "You girls enjoy the rest of your evening."

"Thanks," Candice called as she and Baylee turned to leave.

"Do we have time to run into the candy shop?" Baylee asked as they stepped out into the cool November night.

"Um," Candice hummed, taking her cell phone from her pocket to check the time. "Probably not... and I wanted to pop into that doll store again."

"Well, why don't I just run in to the candy shop for a minute and you run into the doll shop?" Baylee suggested.

Looking to one another, they smiled. "Two birds with one stone!" they chimed in unison.

"Perfect!" Candice exclaimed. "I'll see you back at the square in a few. You only have about fifteen minutes left, okay? I don't know how you could've forgotten your phone tonight."

"I know," Baylee sighed, rolling her eyes in exasperation at her own forgetfulness. "I'll see you back at the square." When Candice quirked one eyebrow in doubt, Baylee giggled, "And on time too! I've never been late to a performance before."

"You've never forgotten your phone before," Candice reminded as she hurried in the opposite direction of where Baylee was headed.

As Baylee hurried toward the Ye Old Candy Shoppe she'd noticed while she was performing earlier, she tucked the small brown paper bag back into her pocket, pushing it in as far as it would go. She already loved her new charm—*loved* it! She couldn't believe Candice had spotted it, because Candice was usually anything but observant of details. She tried to imagine how perfectly it would fit next to the beautiful Christmas tree charm she'd purchased that summer when the Hampton Handbell Ringers had done a stint of performing in Leavenworth, Washington.

"Hi!" she heard someone call. When she looked over to see Malcolm McBride the Third waving to her from across the square, she smiled and tossed a wave as she stepped up onto the steps of Ye Old Candy Shoppe. He was a cute little boy, and his cheeks were rosy with the cold and his own merriment.

"Oh! Excuse me," Baylee apologized as she bumped into someone who was just leaving the candy shop as she was arriving.

"No problem," a deep, masculine voice responded. The man's voice was so sensuously stirring that she immediately looked up.

When Baylee found herself staring into the simmering peacock-green eyes of the phenomenally handsome security guy who had stepped between her and Tate the day before, she could only sputter, "S-sorry."

The gorgeous, black-clad chimney sweep (whose soot-smeared face only served to emphasize the fascinating green of his eyes) smiled, displaying beautiful white teeth, also accentuated by the soot smears.

"Like I said, no problem," he repeated. Baylee blushed when the man rather brazenly studied her from head to toe for a moment. "And don't you look cute in your little Christmas caroler outfit," he said.

Baylee's shock and awe at standing so near the handsome chimney sweep was instantly replaced with humiliation as she realized how silly she must look to him—all dressed in her red velvet and gold trim. At least she wasn't carrying her bells or some stupid thing. Yet as she stood before the good-looking chimney sweep, complete with a chimney brush propped over one shoulder and a raggedy black top hat sitting on his head, she couldn't help but smile.

Furthermore, before she could stop herself, she said, "You too." He smiled again, his green eyes sparkling with amusement as she stammered, "I-I mean…you look good in your chimney sweep togs…because, of course, you're not wearing a caroler's dress…uh… costume and stuff."

He chuckled, and the sound of it caused the back of Baylee's neck to warm with pleasure.

"I'm Justice Kincaid, by the way," he said, offering a hand to her. Baylee smiled as she glanced at his hand to see he wore knitted, black, fingerless gloves.

"I'm Baylee Cabot," she countered as she accepted his hand. The moment the man's hand touched hers, however, she wished she'd been wearing her gloves—for such a wonderfully warming heat passed from his hand to melt into hers that she thought her knees might melt too.

He smiled again and kept hold of Baylee's hand as he asked, "Baylee the handbell ringer, huh?"

"Yeah," she managed. "And Justice the chimney sweep, right?"

"Absolutely," he confirmed. Baylee's breath caught in her throat a moment. Absolutely? *Absolutely* was Baylee's word of choice when it came to offering assurance. The fact that the way-better-looking-than-any-man-in-Hollywood faux chimney sweep would use her word—well, it startled her for some reason.

"You guys are awesome," he said, shaking Baylee out of her astonished stupor. She was bathing, shoulder-deep, in the fact that he still hadn't released her hand. "When you guys performed 'Carol of the Bells' a while ago…" He feigned a shiver and said, "Wow! It was seriously incredible."

"Thank you," she responded, managing to remember the way Mr. Hampton always insisted the members of his handbell ringers accept compliments as graciously as possible. "I-I'm glad you enjoyed it. It's my favorite Christmas carol…well, that and 'Silent Night.'"

"Really?" Justice Kincaid asked, arching one dark eyebrow. "Mine too. I mean…my favorites in the true-meaning-of-Christmas genre, that is. Otherwise I'm always down with 'White Christmas.'"

Baylee giggled, amused by his way of mixing proper speech with urban slang. "I love that one too," she offered, smiling so hard her cheeks hurt. She couldn't believe he was talking to her. She couldn't believe he was still holding her hand!

She wondered how many women had stood in front of this Justice Kincaid guy wishing he would turn out to be their own Mr. Right—just the way she was wishing it right then. *Probably a million*, was her final determination.

Justice grinned, and his eyes seemed to heat up their simmering to something closer to a boil. "We should do hot chocolate sometime, you and me," he suggested.

"The way they do lunch in L.A.?" she giggled.

"Absolutely," he laughed. "Is it a date then? Maybe one night this week? When do you take your dinner break tomorrow night?"

Was he really asking her out—sort of? Did he really mean it? Baylee was fearful that he didn't—that maybe he was just messing with her. But she decided to take a chance anyway—come humiliation or heavenly bliss.

"Um…eight o'clock," she answered. She held her breath, waiting for his response—for his rejection or acceptance.

"Cool. I'll just schedule my break for that same time," he said. "Wanna just meet right here tomorrow night at eight?"

"Sure. That'll be great."

Justice Kincaid's smile broadened again. "Yes…it will," he said. "I'll see you tomorrow night then." He paused a moment, still holding her hand in his and adding, "Well, I'll see you tonight too…all night until the place closes, in fact." He leaned forward, in a low voice, whispering, "You just won't see me. We chimney sweeps are sneaky that way."

"I bet," was all Baylee could think to say.

Releasing her hand, Justice touched the brim of his raggedy black top hat. "Until tomorrow night then, Miss Cabot." Then he stepped around her, disappearing into the pine bough-slathered, cobble-stoned street of Camden Town 1843.

CHAPTER THREE

Justice smiled as he watched the handbell ringers—as he listened to their incredible performance of "Jesu, Joy of Man's Desiring." It was incredible—the peace and calm that seeped into his skin as he listened. And, of course, his favorite little handbell ringer looked as radiant as starlight.

Maybe his asking her out for hot chocolate without even knowing her yet would seem hasty to most people—but he wasn't most people. Justice knew the importance of truly living every second of God-given life. His own life had almost been snuffed out—well, shot out, blown out, or whatever someone wanted to call it. And the moment he'd finally woken up in the hospital to find he hadn't been killed by the crash of the CH-47F Chinook or the IED that had exploded near the crash survivors, Justice swore to himself that he would never let one moment of life pass him by without living it to the fullest.

He nodded, assuring himself he'd done the right thing in already approaching Baylee Cabot, the pretty little red-velvet-draped handbell ringer. Everything about her lured him in—drew him like some awaiting destiny. He would've been an idiot to ignore the feelings she provoked in him. And so, tomorrow night, he'd have hot chocolate with her—treat her to dinner and get to know her better—see if she even wanted to get to know him better.

Raising his binoculars, he quickly scanned the crowds below for anything or anyone who might appear suspicious. It was going to be difficult to keep his mind on his work when the little handbell ringing caroler was always in his sights—but he could do it. It's what he'd done for a very long time.

As the Hampton Handbell Ringers and Carolers began a vocal performance of "God Rest Ye, Merry Gentlemen," Baylee found her attention drawn to the rooftops of the Dickens Village. Her performer's smile broadened as she saw the shadow-like silhouettes of chimney sweeps against the moon- and starlit sky. Some were standing near chimneys, some were sitting on rooftop ledges, and some were hunkered down. She could tell by their silhouetted stances that many of them were watching the handbell ringers, and she wondered if the dashing, flirtatious, seemingly confident Justice Kincaid was one of them.

She still couldn't believe he'd asked her out—well, asked her to *do hot chocolate* with him. For several minutes after their encounter at the candy shop, she'd wondered if she'd just imagined it all. But she knew she hadn't. He really had asked her out for hot chocolate—and she wondered why. Why her? She wasn't anything super extraordinary—nobody who really stood out in a crowd. Well, maybe at that moment she did—after all, she was dressed in red velvet and white fur, holding handbells, and singing "God Rest Ye, Merry Gentlemen"—but other than that, she was just an average Jane. Not that she had low self-esteem or anything like that—not any worse than any other woman her age, anyway. She knew she was smart and semi-talented—but wasn't everybody?

Baylee decided it didn't matter. For some reason, Justice Kincaid had noticed her and wanted to take her out. She wouldn't look a gift horse in the mouth then—she'd just go with it. In fact, her smile broadened as she thought that, more than go *with* it, she'd go *for* it! In her guts she felt that it wasn't just Justice's sinfully good looks that made the back of her neck tingle with excitement—made her skin warm and goose-bumpy at the same time. He would mean something to her, she was sure of it—and she wouldn't screw it up with self-doubt and fear. Nope. Tomorrow at eight she would just be herself in his company—get to know him and hope that he wanted to get to know her. Oh—and she'd try not to stare at him with her mouth gaping open in awed admiration.

As Mr. Hampton cued the handbell ringers to prepare to perform "Carol of the Birds" with their bells, Baylee wished he'd chosen something a bit livelier—something that might have found the silhouetted chimney sweeps linking their elbows to "step in time." A vision of Dick Van Dyke and Julie Andrews all soot-faced and sitting atop the rooftops of London flashed in her mind and she smiled—thinking she'd like nothing more in that moment than to be up on one of the rooftops of the Dickens Village beside Justice Kincaid, her own charming chimney sweep.

❦

"Just like that?" Candice asked. "He just bumped into you in the candy shop and asked you out for tomorrow night?"

"Can you believe it?" Baylee asked, beaming with delighted anticipation.

Candice sipped her warm apple cider and then shook her head. "Dang! And I had to go trotting off to the doll shop and miss everything."

"Maybe he wouldn't have had the nerve to ask me if you'd been with me, Candice. Think about it like that," Baylee offered.

But Candice rolled her eyes. "An Army Ranger, Baylee? Yeah…I'm sure he would've lacked the nerve to ask you out with someone else watching. Please."

Baylee giggled. "Good point," she admitted. She sighed then, sipped her own warm cider a moment, and then said, "He gets me all tingly and, like…you know…thinking stuff that's crazy."

"Like what?" Candice asked.

Baylee shrugged. "I don't know…like…like maybe he can actually really find me interesting and that maybe it could lead to…you know…"

"A house with a white picket fence?" Candice finished.

Baylee nodded a little. "It's crazy, I know. But even though I've only seen him twice...he really does something weird to me."

Candice smiled and whispered, "My guess is he does something weird to any woman who sees him twice...but that he doesn't ask every one of *them* out to do hot chocolate. So quit wondering why he asked you, and just go for it." Candice sipped her cider and added, "Stranger things have happened than a handbell ringer marrying a chimney sweep Army Ranger. I mean, look at Mrs. Graham at the instrument store."

Baylee laughed then, entirely amused by Candice's example. "I will admit that that might have been stranger."

"Of course it was stranger!" Candice said. "Mrs. Graham is, what, midfifties? And Colton Roberts was, what, *maybe* thirty when they got married? And they met at a scrapbooking store? Okay...a handbell ringer and an Army Ranger is nothing...believe me."

Baylee giggled again. It had been quite a scandal—the fact that Mrs. Graham, the uptight violin teacher (for all outward appearances) at the instrument store next to Mr. Hampton's bell shop, up and eloped with some twenty-something hottie whose mother owned the local scrapbooking store.

"You're talking about Mrs. Graham and her boy-toy again?" Tate interrupted, intruding on Candice and

Baylee's conversation as usual. "Word on the street is he married her for her money."

"She's a violin teacher, Tate," Baylee sighed. "It's not like she's loaded."

But Tate shrugged and said, "I'm just saying... there's got to be some reason he married her."

"He married her because he loves her, you dork," Candice said.

Tate grimaced. "She's like fifty-five or something! Who could love that?"

"Oh my gosh...you are such a butt. I can't even talk to you," Candice grumbled.

"And what brought that up anyway?" Tate asked, ignoring Candice's cut down.

But Candice's temperament was piqued, and even though Baylee warned, "Candice...don't," Candice turned to Tate and said, "We were talking about how you never can tell who the one for you might be. It just so happens that one of the chimney sweeps has asked Baylee out."

Tate frowned at Baylee. "Don't tell me you're getting sucked into that 'fallen hero,' too much muscle and not enough brain thing. Come on, Baylee. I thought you were smarter than that. Those guys are nothing but warmongers. There's nothing to them but guns and testosterone."

"As opposed to the good fashion sense and cowardice that composes you, Tate?" Baylee countered. She couldn't stand Tate! He was so soft and mushy— like a Beanie Baby, only not as cute. And he was cocky, which made everything else she didn't like about him worse.

"Hey, a well-dressed man goes places," Tate argued.

"Then why don't you go somewhere right now?" Candice suggested. She frowned a moment, studying Tate from head to toe. "Why is it you're always in our business anyway, Tate? I've never been able to figure that out."

"Well, someone has to look out for you two," he answered. "I mean, look at you. We've been here one evening, and already Baylee has managed to get snagged by some GI who's only after one thing."

"And what's he after, Tate?" Baylee asked. Her temper was rising—just as her confidence where Justice Kincaid's reasons for asking her out was waning a little.

"Why don't you let me show you, Baylee?" Tate said, unexpectedly taking her waist between his hands and attempting to pull her against him.

But Baylee's knee to his groin region caused him to immediately release her and double over a little. "Don't ever touch me again, Tate," Baylee growled. "And maybe you better tell Mr. Hampton you'll be singing tenor for the rest of the night."

Justice chuckled quietly as he watched Baylee and her friend walk away from the same jerk who had been hassling them in the parking lot the day before.

"She's ain't shy, that's for sure," he chuckled to himself as he continued to peer through his binoculars—this time scanning the different gatherings of people below for any sign of the FBI's Jack the Ripper. "I guess you'll be singing tenor for the rest of the night, you idiot."

He paused in scanning the area below, his smile immediately fading as he watched a black-cloaked figure keeping to the shadows of a nearby alleyway. But when the man tossed something in a trash barrel and returned to the village square and to a vendor's cart selling Christmas puddings, he exhaled the breath he'd been holding. With all the period clothing running around in the Dickens Village, any man wearing a cloak and a top hat looked like Jack the Ripper to Justice.

Lowering his binoculars, he wondered for a minute if he still wanted to be a field agent. An office job wasn't any more boring than standing on a rooftop at night waiting for Jack the Ripper to show up. Still, at least he was outside in the fresh, crisp air.

Shaking his head, he thought to himself that he wasn't ready to give up fieldwork—not yet. He figured the day would come when maybe he wouldn't want to be in the line of fire at all—but it hadn't come yet.

Justice heard Brian's voice on his earpiece and hurried to follow his instructions to check out the alleyway between the bakery and the candy shop. As he stealthily hurried over the rooftops, he was certain that scaling buildings in the dark of night was preferable to working nine to five behind a desk. Yet he wondered how his favorite little caroler would feel about it. Of course, that thought was immediately followed by another. *What the heck does it matter and who is she to cause me to even worry about it?*

Still, as he lay down and adjusted his binoculars to recon the cloaked man in the top hat in the alley, he wondered again what Baylee Cabot would think if she knew what he really did for a living.

❧

"I am *so* tired," Candice yawned as they walked toward the exit gates of the Dickens Village.

The village was closing for the night—finally—and Baylee felt like she could sleep for a week!

"I think this gig might be more taxing than I thought," she said.

"Me too," Candice agreed. "But at least tomorrow night it'll only be six hours. And we don't even have to be here until four, so that's good."

"Plus, I'm sure we'll adjust," Baylee added. It was her attempt to remotivate herself, but she was still more tired than she'd expected.

"You didn't lose your new charm, did you?" Candice asked.

Baylee shook her head but stuffed her hand in her pocket to make sure the little box in the brown paper bag was still there anyway. "Nope. It's safe and sound, and I'm going to put it on my bracelet the minute I get home."

Baylee and Candice were quiet for a moment as they stepped out of 1843 London and back into real life. Baylee inhaled a breath of the cool night air. The scent of wood smoke, cinnamon, and pine boughs still laced the night, and she smiled.

"It's such a dreamy place, isn't it?" she asked Candice.

"The Dickens Village? Totally! As tired as I am, I hate to leave it," Candice replied.

"And since it is such a dreamy place," Baylee began, "you don't think I only dreamed that Justice Kincaid asked me out, do you?"

Candice laughed. "No, stupid! He really did." But Candice's brows drew together in a frown as she added, "Though I wasn't there to see it happen. But just because I didn't see it doesn't mean you dreamed it." She grumbled and playfully slapped Baylee on one velvet-covered shoulder. "See? Now you've got me doing it. Of course he asked you out!"

Then, as if in answer to Baylee's doubts, she heard Justice's voice call out, "Hey, Baylee," from behind them.

Stopping in their tracks, both Baylee and Candice spun around to see a very handsome chimney sweep striding toward them.

"Holy cow! Maybe we *are* dreaming!" Candice whispered. "I swear I've never seen a guy that handsome in real life."

"Shhh," Baylee softly scolded as she watched Justice approach.

"Hi," he said as he stopped before them. He looked from Baylee to Candice, offered a strong hand, and said, "I'm Justice Kincaid."

Taking his hand, Candice smiled and said, "Candice Jones."

"It's nice to meet you," he said, smiling.

"You too," Candice managed to answer, though Baylee knew Candice well enough to know when her friend was entirely rattled.

"I just wanted to make sure you're still available to do hot chocolate tomorrow night," Justice said, addressing Baylee.

"Oh, yeah! Absolutely!" she answered, knowing she was way too exuberant.

"Good," he said. "I'll meet you by the fountain. But I think we should get something to eat too. I won't last the rest of the night on just hot chocolate, okay?"

"Absolutely!" Baylee exclaimed again. "I'm really looking forward to it."

"Me too," Justice confirmed. He looked up a moment then, beyond them. "Where are you girls parked? I don't feel right about you walking out into this dark parking lot alone like this."

"Just over there," Baylee said, gesturing to where her car and Candice's were parked.

"Well, I'll see you girls to your cars all the same," he said. "I'm old school, you see. I don't believe women should have to walk to their cars alone in the dark or change flat tires."

"How very chivalrous, Mr. Kincaid," Candice said.

"No. Just paranoid," he answered.

Baylee felt a shock of excitement travel up her spine as Justice placed a hand at her lower back and nodded toward the cars. "Come on, ladies. Let's get you safely to your cars and on your way home."

"Thank you," Baylee said, again grateful for all the nagging Mr. Hampton had given the handbell ringers about gracious acceptance.

Once they were to the cars, Baylee smiled when Justice opened her car door for her after she'd pushed the unlock button her key. "Wow! You *are* quite a charming chimney sweep, aren't you?"

"Not really," he said. Then, smiling, he added, "Have a good night, Baylee. See you tomorrow," and closed her door for her.

As she drove out of the Dickens Village parking lot, Baylee Cabot was on cloud nine! She wondered briefly what was so special about cloud number nine that everyone who was there was euphoric. But the trivial question quickly left her thoughts, for nothing would ever again hold her attention the way Justice Kincaid did. Of that she was sure!

❧

Baylee's apartment was quiet—except for the soft, sweet sounds of Aureole's harps, dulcimers, and flutes playing via their *Christmas Wishes* CD. She snuffed out the flame of her pine- and peppermint-scented candle and turned off all the lights in her bedroom, save the strand of colored mini Christmas lights wound around the post of the lamp that stood by her bed.

Sitting down on her bed, she gently removed the beautiful silver Victorian caroler charm from its pretty velvet box and began to attach it to her special charm bracelet. She didn't have very many charms on her sterling charm bracelet yet—only the Leavenworth

Christmas tree, a pretty silver-handled gold bell charm, and the pirate ship charm she'd fallen in love with in a shop in Boston.

Carefully Baylee attached the caroler charm to her bracelet and then held it up toward the mini Christmas lights and watched the colors they beamed sparkle on the pretty charms.

"Perfect!' she sighed with contentment. It was late, and she was tired, but there was always time for one more delight in life—at least to Baylee's way of thinking there was.

Still, fatigue did get the best of her, and she put the charm bracelet back in her jewelry box and snuggled down into her warm, comfortable bed. The CD would play a few more songs and then turn off on its own, and the Christmas lights were so soothing that Baylee decided to leave them on as well.

She was amazed that she was so relaxed. The date she had scheduled with Justice Kincaid normally would've found her wound up like top, but she was astonishingly calm. Oh, it wasn't like the image of Justice that kept swaying back and forth in her mind wasn't distracting, as well as exciting. It was just that it soothed her somehow too—as if he were right there in the room watching over and protecting her. It was weird, but the whole thing was weird anyway. Baylee had never accepted a date with a guy she hadn't known for at least a couple of weeks. Well, she'd never accepted one until Justice Kincaid had asked. But what woman in her right mind would've turned down a date with that piece of French silk pie, huh?

She thought then of how the soot on his face made his peacock-green eyes all the more alluring. And, yes, that's what they were—alluring. As she gazed at the small colored lights wrapped around her lamppost, she thought that maybe Justice's eyes were more the color of the warm-lit Christmas green bulbs on the string of lights. Either way, whether peacock-green or mini-Christmas-lights green, Justice's eyes were definitely something a girl could get lost in.

Smiling, Baylee thought that Justice Kincaid's arms were also something a girl could get lost in—and his smile—and his muscles—and his hair—and the sound of his voice…

CHAPTER FOUR

Baylee may have fallen asleep easily enough, but the next morning she was so stirred up she could hardly concentrate on anything! All day long she found herself fidgeting, impatient, and nervous. And when four o'clock finally rolled around and the Hampton Handbell Ringers began performing in the Dickens Village square, all Baylee could think about was whether Justice Kincaid was perched up on one of the rooftops watching her. She was so entirely distracted, wondering where Justice was stationed and why in the world it was taking eight p.m. so long to arrive, that she was constantly worried she'd make a mistake while ringing—but she didn't, and time ticked by as slowly as a sloth could swim through molasses. She watched the sun set while the group sang "Good King Wenceslas" and enjoyed a cup of mulled cider with Candice during a short break, and still all she could think of was seeing Justice—of being with him. She knew it was crazy to be so fixated—insane! But that didn't change the truth of it.

At long, long, *long* last, the big hand on the large clock in the Dickens Village clock tower began to inch toward twelve as the little hand settled on eight, and then—he was there! Baylee spied Justice Kincaid standing near the fountain in the square, smiling as he watched the troupe perform. He was there! He was there waiting for her! Her heart swelled with such raging anticipation she could hardly contain her delight. She knew her smile was way too big to be appropriate when the group was singing "Coventry Carol," but she couldn't help it. Justice was waiting for her—for *her*—Baylee Cabot!

As the carol ended and the onlookers began to applaud, Baylee barely managed to wait for Mr. Hampton to dismiss them before hurrying off to meet Justice.

"Hi," Justice greeted as she approached. Oh, his smile was simply over the moon!

"Hi," she greeted in return.

"Are you ready?" he asked.

"Absolutely," she answered (too enthusiastically, of course).

"I was thinking we'd go to the place that does the old-fashioned ham and potato thing," he suggested. "What do you think?"

Baylee shrugged. "I don't know anything about it...but I like ham, and I like potatoes."

"Should be good then," he chuckled.

As they walked toward the little restaurant near the bakery, Baylee tried to breathe evenly, but it was difficult. She wasn't only nervous and excited about being with Justice; she was nervous and unsettled by the way people looked at them and grinned—by the way women looked at Justice, their eyes lighting up like Christmas trees.

Baylee figured she and Justice probably did provide quite a sight—the Victorian Christmas caroler, all bedecked in red velvet and white fur, and the sooty, and outrageously handsome, chimney sweep with the peacock-green eyes and the tattered top hat.

They entered the restaurant (Baylee blushing with delight as Justice opened the door, allowing her to enter first), and in minutes, a waitress had seated them at a small table next to a window. The waitress, dressed in the perfect period clothing, handed them menus and left them.

"Mmm. I'm starving," Justice mumbled as he studied the menu. "You know, I never really realize how hungry I am until I start reading a list of good things to eat."

Baylee smiled. "Me neither," she agreed. "And, look, they do have hot chocolate. I was worried for a moment that they wouldn't have any and I'd start into chocolate withdrawal right here in front of you."

"It's that bad, huh?" he chuckled.

Baylee nodded. "You should've seen me scrounging around in my baking cabinet, hoping to find a stray chocolate chip or something last night before I went to bed."

Justice chuckled again, and she silently scolded

herself for being so forthcoming about her passion for chocolate. He'd think she was an idiot for sure.

Smiling, however, he studied her a moment, his unsettling green gaze warming her from her insides out.

"I like hot chocolate too," he said, returning his attention to his menu. "And I'm not just saying that to try to impress you." He grinned, adding, "Though I'm not sure I need chocolate enough to recon a rogue chocolate chip from the cabinet."

Baylee giggled. "Well, now you know my worst secret," she sighed. "So I guess there's no reason for me to be nervous anymore."

Wow, Justice thought. If rooting around in a cabinet looking for chocolate chips were Baylee Cabot's worst secret, then he hoped opposites really did attract as strongly as the old cliché claimed. He grinned, thinking his worst secrets would probably set her hair on fire.

He looked up, smiling with amusement as he watched her considering her menu. Her pretty forehead was furrowed with a frown, her lips were pursed to one side, and one slender index finger rested at her rosy cheek.

"Looks pretty straightforward to me," she mumbled. Then, rather dramatically closing her menu with a contented sigh, she smiled at him and said, "Ham and fried potatoes for me." Her smile broadened, and her brown eyes twinkled warmly as she added, "With the dinner roll, of course! Maybe I'll ask for two." She frowned again, adding, "Do you think they'd get mad if I asked for two?"

Justice smiled and answered, "I'm sure they won't get mad." She was too funny! He'd already decided that this was the best, most enjoyable dinner date he'd ever been on, and it hadn't even been ten minutes yet.

"So," Baylee said, folding her arms and plopping them down on the top of the table. "Is it true that all you chimney sweep security guys are ex-military?"

And here it came—the moment when Justice would begin to determine what the pretty little bell ringer's opinion of certain things was.

"Yep," he answered with trepidation rising in his chest. "Every one of us."

She smiled at him, dispelling much of his anxiety over what she would think of his having been in the military. In fact, it subsided almost instantly. "And judging from your license plate...I'm guessing you were Army," she baited.

He chuckled. "Judging by the *vanity* plates my grandma had put on that truck before she gave it to me, you mean? Yes."

Her eyes widened, and she giggled. "Wow! Your grandma *gave* you a truck?"

"Yep. When I was discharged," he began to explain. He folded his menu and set it aside, having decided on the ham, fried potatoes, and two dinner rolls himself. "Grandma has always spoiled me rotten...and since my Grandpa died last year, I haven't had the heart to argue with her. The truck was actually my grandpa's, and when he died she ordered those stupid vanity license plates and gave his truck to me. It was only, like, maybe three months old when he died, and she was determined I should have it." He looked up to see Baylee smiling at him and couldn't help but smile himself. He shrugged and added, "What's a grandson to do, right? And besides…she gave me the payment too."

Baylee giggled. "Wow! That's a nice truck…so I'm sure the payment is nice as well."

"Absolutely," Justice chuckled.

"And as for the license plates, I think you *should* be proud of your service. Besides, people need to be reminded that conflicts and the soldiers who deal with them really do exist. That's half of what's wrong with this country today. Nobody has had to worry about their freedom being stripped away in far too long."

"Agreed," Justice said.

"My daddy is a Gulf War vet, and my grandpa did four tours in Vietnam, so I get it," she said. "Probably not as much as I would have seventy years or so ago, but I do get it." Her smile broadened, and the light in her eyes flashed with approval. "So I like the plates your grandma had put on your truck. And furthermore, thank you for your service to me and my country, Mr. Justice Kincaid."

Justice was far more than just merely impressed; he was touched emotionally. It wasn't very often that a young person thanked him for his service—especially a beautiful young bell-ringing caroler. He could see that she was thoroughly sincere in thanking him—that she truly meant what she said.

"Well, you're welcome," he mumbled, smiling at her and blushing a little with humility. "It's not very often a pretty young thing like you thanks a beat-up old Army Ranger like me for his service." He breathed a quiet laugh and added, "I think I love you already."

Sure—Baylee knew he was kidding. She knew Justice was only expressing how rare it was these days for a military veteran to be thanked for his service. But even though she knew he didn't *really* think he loved her, the sound of his voice saying the words sent a wave of butterflies whirling around in her stomach.

She didn't know how to respond—couldn't think of anything to say. Therefore, her mouth made the call and said, "I hope so."

The waitress returned, setting two small tankards of water on the table and rescuing Baylee from any further flustering. "Are you ready to order?" she asked.

Saved by the waitress, Baylee thought.

"I think so," Justice answered. Looking to Baylee, however, he asked, "Are you sticking with the ham and fried potatoes?" even though she'd told him before that she was.

"Yes," she assured him.

"She'll be having the ham and fried potatoes, but will you please add an extra dinner roll to that?" he began.

"Of course, sir," the waitress assured him. "And for you, sir?"

"I'll have the same…including two rolls instead of just one, okay?" Justice grinned and winked at Baylee, and again the butterflies in her stomach whirled around again.

"Of course," the waitress said. "Anything else? Would you like something to drink?"

"Actually, yes…two hot chocolates as well," Justice answered.

The waitress smiled. "Our hot chocolate is the best in the village," she said, "even if I do say so myself. Would you like the soft peppermint cocoa stirrers too?"

"Are they the ones with the little holes in the middle so you can suck your hot chocolate through them?" Justice asked.

Baylee smiled. He knew about soft peppermint sticks in hot chocolate? How adorable! Maybe he really did like hot chocolate as much as she did. Or nearly as much, anyway.

"Yes, they are," the waitress giggled.

"Then I definitely want one," Justice assured her. "Baylee?" he asked, looking to her.

"Absolutely," she answered.

"All right then," the waitress began, "that's two ham and fried potato dinners, with two dinner rolls each." She smiled and winked at Justice. "And two hot chocolates complete with peppermint stirrers."

"That's it, exactly," Justice affirmed.

"Well then, it shouldn't be too long on the dinners. Would you like your hot chocolate now or later?"

"Both," Justice answered.

Baylee giggled as he winked at her again. It was like he could read her mind where hot chocolate was concerned.

"I'll have the first round brought right out to you then," the waitress affirmed.

"Thank you."

Baylee watched as even their waitress, who she gauged to be in her late fifties, blushed under Justice's gaze. "You're welcome, and let me know if there's anything else I can do for you," she said before leaving them alone once more.

Baylee studied Justice a moment, arching one brow with suspicion. "Do you *really* like hot chocolate that much? Or are you just trying to make me feel better?"

He smiled his goose-bump-inducing smile. "I really do love hot chocolate," he insisted. He leaned forward, however, and in a lowered, very provocative voice added, "But I would do anything to make you feel better too."

Baylee giggled—blushed as well. "Are all you Army Rangers so charming?"

"You mean chimney sweeps?" he asked.

Again she giggled. "Yeah. Are all you chimney sweeps so charming?"

He shrugged. "You know what they say—chimney sweeps are good luck, right? Isn't good luck a sort of charm or spell?" He grinned. "Here," he said, offering his hand to her across the table. "Shake my hand. It's supposed to be good luck, according to Dick Van Dyke anyway."

Baylee laughed and accepted his hand. He shook hers firmly and then released it. Smiling at her, he then asked, "Do you feel charmed with good luck now?"

While it was true her palm was still tingling with the delight of having touched him, she didn't know if she felt any luckier that she had a moment ago. She already felt lucky to be with him—lucky that he'd even taken notice of her, lucky that he'd asked her out, lucky all the way around where he was concerned. Therefore, she didn't know what feeling luckier would've felt like because she was already euphoric.

"Well? Do you?" Justice pressed, teasing her. She knew he was teasing, because his peacock-green eyes were flashing like burning emeralds.

"I don't know," she answered honestly. "I was already feeling pretty lucky today."

He wrinkled his handsome brow, feigning concern. "Well, what's next then?" He pretended to be thoughtful. "Ah, yes. Blow me a kiss. Blowing me a kiss is supposed to be lucky as well."

"According to Dick Van Dyke," Baylee giggled.

"Absolutely," he chuckled.

"So you want me to blow you a kiss now? Is that it?" she asked.

He shrugged broad shoulders. "Well, you can just lean over here and give me a kiss…but we've only known each other, what, a total of twenty minutes?"

Baylee blushed and glanced away. She saw the older couple sitting at a table near them, smiling at her with understanding—and delight.

"Come on," Justice urged. "Blow me a kiss and see if you feel luckier." He winked at her. "I've always wanted a kiss from a pretty bell-ringing caroler girl."

Quickly, Baylee kissed her fingers, bending her hand toward Justice and blowing the kiss to him. "Okay. There. Are you happy?"

"Yep," he said, grinning at her. "And do you feel good luck washing over you now?"

At that moment, a busboy arrived, carrying a tray with two tankards sitting on it. Each had a peppermint stick sticking out of it.

"Here you go, sir…ma'am," the young man said as he sat a tankard of hot cocoa on the table in front of Baylee and then another in front of Justice.

"Thank you," Justice said, though his gaze never deviated from Baylee.

"You're welcome," the young man said as he walked away.

"Well?" Justice asked. The arrival of the hot chocolate did nothing to distract him from his previous question. "Do you feel lucky now or not?"

Smiling, Baylee reached out and pulled the tankard of hot chocolate closer to her. Stirring the hot chocolate with the long peppermint stick protruding from it, she smiled and said, "The hot chocolate arrived, didn't it? How much more luck could I hope for?"

Justice's smile broadened. Yep—he'd known her all of twenty minutes, and already he liked her more than he'd liked anyone in a very, very long time. He watched her sip her hot chocolate through the peppermint stick, thinking that her lips probably tasted pretty sweet right about then.

"So," she began, looking up at him, slowly stirring her cocoa. "Why did you leave the military? Rangers… that's, like, a big commitment. Most of you guys just don't up and quit, right?"

Usually when people asked Justice about his military service, he was instantly overwhelmed with the need to put up his guard. He more often than not felt defensive and was always waiting for the negative shoe to drop. But none of the usual feelings welled up in him when Baylee asked him about it. It was a strange sensation—not feeling immediately self-protective.

"I…uh…I was wounded," he answered. He hadn't even taken pause to think about what to tell her and what not to. He'd simply answered.

"Thus the Purple Heart?" she inquired.

"One of them, yes," he admitted. When she didn't say anything else, he knew she was waiting for particulars. He figured it wouldn't hurt to give her a few—not too many and no grisly details. But if he wanted to get to know her better and wanted her to get to know him…

"We'd picked up some Navy SEALS that had gotten…that were backed into a corner, so to speak. The Chinook we were in was shot down, and when we crashed—once we'd gotten the survivors out and dragged from the wreckage—an IED exploded and blew us all to hell. I woke up in the base hospital with enough serious injuries to find me discharged and unemployed."

Justice was surprised when he glanced up to see excess moisture brimming in Baylee's eyes. The sight of her sympathy for him pricked his heart and caused a pinching sensation in his chest.

"How awful," she mumbled. She looked down to the hot chocolate she had once again begun stirring with the peppermint stick. "And I'm sure that's the Easy Reader version too. Isn't it?"

Justice shrugged. "Probably."

He watched as she studied him for a moment, knowing she was looking for signs of lingering injury.

"Well, you look robust enough," she said once she realized she'd been staring at him.

Justice smiled. "Well, you haven't seen me naked," he said in a lowered voice.

The entire surface of Baylee's body blushed. Of course she hadn't seen him naked! What did he mean by that? It only took her a moment to calm herself, however—only a moment to realize that, though Justice Kincaid obviously had all his limbs and a wickedly handsome face, there was a profound amount of flesh, bone, and other parts of the human body that weren't visible to the world—when he was fully clothed, anyway.

"And here we go," the waitress said as she arrived

with two plates of steaming food. She placed one in front of Baylee, the other in front of Justice. "And two rolls each," she added, smiling.

"Thank you," Justice said.

"Let me know if you need anything else," the waitress offered.

"We will. Thank you," Baylee promised.

"Mmm. It smells good," Justice mumbled as he inhaled the steam coming off his plate.

But Baylee was still rattled. She knew Justice was giving her merely a drop in the bucket of whatever had gone on to injure him enough to find him discharged from the Army—from the Army Rangers. She tried to keep more tears from welling in her eyes, but her heart was aching at wondering what he'd truly endured.

"So they patched you up and sent you on your way?" she asked as she used her knife and fork to cut a piece of ham.

"Yep," he answered. He shrugged. "I had the option, of course…a desk job, so to speak. But if it was a desk job or discharge—"

"You chose discharge." He nodded. She wouldn't press him further. She knew that it was important to wait until someone like Justice was ready to offer details of their service of their own accord. At least that's how it had always been with her father and grandfather. If he wanted her to know more, he'd tell her—someday.

"And now you're a security guard," she stated. She frowned a moment, looking up at him. "What company do you guys work for anyway? I mean…why would the Dickens Village need security guards with the backgrounds you guys all have?"

Baylee thought for a moment that the bite of potatoes Justice had just taken had gotten stuck in his throat when he coughed a little. But he took a drink of water and answered, "Well, we're not just a security force. We're more specialized than that. I'm a field agent, actually...for a bureau that...you know...does special assignments like this sometimes."

"For a bureau?" she asked. "You mean like the Federal Bureau of Investigation...the FBI or MI6, the CIA, or something?"

Justice smiled. "You're thinking of James Bond and Tom Cruise stuff," he chuckled. "I'm more like...oh, you know...mall cop."

Baylee giggled. "Oh, you are not," she playfully argued. "Mall cops don't carry the kinds of weapons you guys were packing at the orientation."

"Packing?" Justice said, grinning.

Baylee shrugged. "Isn't that's what it's called?"

"Armed is what I usually call it...but I guess packing works too," he laughed. He paused to take a bite of ham and a sip of hot chocolate, and then he said, "Maybe I just like weaponry."

Baylee nodded. "Most guys usually do. When my brother was little, he'd always sneak into my mom's sewing room and get her hot glue gun out to play with. He could make anything into a gun. I suppose you relate to that."

"Mmm hmmm," Justice confirmed. "But I was

into the sword thing too. I started out with the old paper towel roll things—you know, the cardboard tube left over when you've finished the roll?"

Baylee giggled at the thought of a cute little Justice Kincaid playing with empty paper towel rolls.

"Then I graduated to the big ones," he continued. "You know, Christmas wrapping paper size." He smiled and chuckled to himself. "Those were awesome!"

"I can imagine," Baylee teased.

"But then, the Christmas I was four…" he sighed.

He paused and didn't continue, so Baylee prodded, "Yeah? The Christmas you were four…"

"That was the Christmas I got my first *real* weapon," he answered, gazing off to one corner of the room, reminiscently.

"At four years old?" Baylee exclaimed. She was mortified! What parent would give their child a weapon at only four years old?

"Yep," Justice confirmed, however. "That Christmas I got my very first light saber."

Baylee nearly choked on the potatoes she'd been swallowing. Bursting into laughter, she squealed, "Light saber? So it was a toy weapon they gave you?"

"It was a light saber, and it was as real to me as any light saber any other Jedi Knight ever owned," Justice explained. He laughed for a moment, obviously entertained by Baylee's amusement. "It was one of those plastic ones, you know, with the collapsible light saber part? Only it had batteries in the grip, so it really did light up." He shook his head and sighed. "Man! That was an awesome weapon. I still have it somewhere." He drank some hot chocolate and then asked, "And what about you? Have you always been a singing bell ringer?"

Baylee giggled—giggled because of the irony of what she was about to say. "Well, it seems that you and I both enjoyed profound Christmas gifts at an early age…because I received my first bell when I was the same age you were when you got your first *weapon*."

"Seriously?" he asked, chuckling.

Baylee nodded. "Yep. I had seen handbell ringers on TV one year and immediately began begging for my own set of handbells. When I didn't let up on the begging, I guess my parents began to realize that I really did want to play the bells, so they began buying them for me." She paused, laughing for a moment at the memory of her father wearing earmuffs whenever he was working in his office at home. "I must've drove them nuts now that I think about it."

Justice laughed too. "I'm sure of it. Especially if you only received one at a time. Imagine…the same bell…the same note…over and over and over until you received another one."

Baylee giggled. "Yeah, I kind of feel bad for them now."

"You probably should," Justice agreed. He ate a couple of bites of ham and then asked, "And do you plan on ringing and singing forever? Is that something a person can really do as a career for their whole life?"

Baylee shrugged. "Yeah. But there's a lot of travel

involved usually, especially around the holidays," she explained. "It's not so bad now, especially this year when we're sticking close to home most of the time. But when I, you know, have my own family and stuff…I hope then I can just teach music…maybe start a little handbell ringing club or something—you know, to make sure the art doesn't become extinct."

So she wanted a family of her own, did she? Justice liked that. In fact, the same weird sensation he'd had the day he first sort-of met her was washing over him again—the intense warmth at the back of his neck and the feeling like he should already know everything about her. The difference was that this time the weird sensation didn't creep him out the way it had before. It pleased him—made him feel satisfied or content or something.

"Baylee's Baby Handbell Ringers, huh?" he teased. He laughed, adding, "You know, you could recruit all the toddlers in your neighborhood, give them each one bell, and teach them to drive their parents nuts."

Baylee laughed too. "Absolutely!"

Once they'd both laughed a moment longer, Justice said, "But, really…I love to listen to you guys perform. It's awesome."

"Thank you," she said, graciously accepting his compliment. She blushed, however, and she wondered if she'd simply been taught to politely recognize compliments.

Something caught Justice's eye then as Baylee lifted

her fork to her mouth—a bracelet at her wrist. "What's that?" he asked.

Baylee finished putting a bite of food in her mouth, chewed, swallowed, and then looked at her wrist. "You mean the bracelet?" she asked, setting her fork down.

"Yeah."

"I know," she said, shaking her head. "I forgot to take it off today before I came to work, and Mr. Hampton had a fit when he saw it…because it can interfere with ringing. But I don't want to put it in my pocket and lose it or something."

Reaching out and taking hold of her hand, Justice began to inspect the bracelet. It was obviously a charm bracelet, and it was loaded with charms.

"So each one means something?" he asked, taking hold of a silver snowflake charm and studying it.

"Well, kind of," she answered. "This is my Christmas charm bracelet. See? All the charms are kind of wintery and Christmassy?"

Justice touched another charm—a Christmas wreath.

"I've always loved charm bracelets…though I don't know why," she explained. "I have several of them made from these kinds of charms. But the feather in my cap will be the sterling silver one I'm slowly working on… very slowly working on. I only have a few charms for it. In fact, I bought one here yesterday."

When she paused, Justice looked up to see her smiling at him—her beautiful brown eyes entirely alight with excitement.

"It was a Victorian Christmas caroler that my friend came across in the little jewelry store here," she finished.

"Well, how appropriate is that, right?" Justice offered, studying another charm on her bracelet. In truth, he wasn't all that interested in each individual charm—but he liked the way it felt to hold her little hand in his—to touch her wrist. It made him wish he were a charm on her bracelet so that he could lie against her warm, soft skin for a while.

"If you're worried about it," he began, "I can keep it safe for you until you're finished tonight." He smiled, adding, "I *am* a security guard, after all."

"I wouldn't want to inconvenience you," Baylee lied. Of *course* she wanted to inconvenience him with taking care of her bracelet! Any excuse to see him again was wonderful. And besides, the idea of his having possession of something of hers for a while—of knowing he'd touched it and kept it safe for her—it was a sort of titillating feeling.

"It wouldn't be an inconvenience," he said as he began to fumble with the bracelet clasp. "I don't want you getting in trouble with your boss again. Then you might not be able to meet me for dinner tomorrow night during our break, right?"

"Tomorrow night?" Baylee squeaked as her heart leapt with delight in her bosom.

"Sure," Justice said as the clasp released the bracelet into his hand. She watched as he tucked it into the inside pocket of his tailcoat. "You wouldn't mind another hour in my company, would you? Another free meal?"

Would she mind? Was he nuts? Of course she wouldn't mind! It was like a dream come true, his asking her to dinner again in a roundabout way.

"Of course not," she managed to answer. The strangely blissful joy in her heart was fast spreading to her entire body. "But you can't pay tomorrow too. Let's at least go dutch."

"I'll think about it," he said, smiling at her again.

And, oh, that smile! Baylee was sure she was going to melt into a puddle right there in her seat. Why on earth was she there with him? Why had he asked her to go out? What could a man like Justice Kincaid possibly see in a simple girl like her? He'd been around the world, seen battle, been wounded. Terror, adventure, harm—all those things had been a part of his life. He was a hero—a real, live American hero! How in the world had she managed to capture his attention at all?

Baylee began to wonder if maybe there was something else at work—some sort of magical charm that existed within the gates and walls of the Dickens Village. She wondered if outside the village it would dissipate—leave Justice wondering why he'd wasted an hour in the company of someone as pathetically average as Baylee was in comparison to him. She hoped not—prayed not. And yet it was all so unbelievable!

"I need more hot chocolate already," Justice mumbled. "How about you?"

Baylee glanced into her tankard, noting that it was almost empty. "Yep. Mine's gone as well."

"Well then, I'll order round two," he said, smiling. "Maybe I can get the waitress to shake my chimney sweep hand and she'll give us each two peppermint straws this time, huh?"

Baylee giggled as Justice stood up from his chair and strode across the room to talk to the waitress.

"That's one handsome chimney sweep you've got there, love," the elderly woman sitting at the nearby table said.

"Yes, it is," Baylee giggled as the woman's elderly husband winked at her with understanding.

"They're supposed to be good luck, you know," the elderly woman added. "So how's your luck running so far this evening?"

"Astonishingly good," Baylee answered as she watched Justice sauntering back toward her.

Taking his seat again, Justice asked, "So what's your friend doing for dinner tonight since you're busy with me?"

Baylee shrugged. "She went to another place with some of the others in the group."

Justice grinned. "Well, how about this? If I hook your friend up with a chimney sweep dinner date every night next week, can I have you for dinner every night next week?"

Baylee blushed—giggled when the elderly lady at the table next to theirs answered, "Of course you can!"

"Thank you, ma'am," Justice laughed, winking at

74

the old woman. "I'll take care of it then," he said to Baylee. "What's your friend's name again?"

"Candice," she answered.

"She seems like an adventurous young lady… so I think I'll start her out with Tristan," he said thoughtfully.

"You don't have to entertain my friends for me, you know," Baylee said. Lowering her voice, she bravely, and rather brazenly, added, "You can have me for dinner every night next week without going to all that trouble."

Justice chuckled. He liked that she'd found the nerve to say what she'd said. He could tell by her blush that it took a bit more courage than she was used to exerting when communicating with a man. He liked her all the more for her bravery.

"Well, how about I have you for dinner every night and ease your mind about whether or not your friend is having fun too? Okay?" he said.

"Okay," she said, blushing again.

Justice chuckled when he heard the elderly woman at the table next to them sigh with contentment. Baylee giggled a little too, and he realized the sound of it made his smile broaden.

"Here you go," the waitress said, setting two new tankards of hot chocolate on the table. "Enjoy."

"We will, thank you," Justice said, indicating with a nod to Baylee that she should note the two peppermint stick straws in each tankard.

Life was too short to waste even one moment. When a man found what he wanted, there was no reason to mess around with squandering time. Something was telling him that this girl was what he'd been looking for—something that caused the back of his neck to heat up, caused his insides to twist and churn and feel good all at the same time. Therefore, he wouldn't dillydally, as his grandmother would say. Justice Kincaid decided then and there that he wouldn't let any of the unpredictable IEDs that life could throw at a man keep him from pursuing the sweetest little bell-ringing caroler he could ever have dreamt of—keep him from winning her, from having her for dinner every night for the rest of his life.

CHAPTER FIVE

"Wow," Justice said as he closed the Veterans Day card and returned it to its envelope. "I-I...I don't know what to say," he stammered. "Thank you, Baylee."

Baylee smiled when Justice didn't look up to her right away—when he did and she saw the moisture of tender emotion in his eyes.

"Thank *you*, Justice," she countered. "Though I should've given every one of you guys a Veterans Day card." She sighed, wishing she'd had the time, the money, and the information to send every military veteran in the world a card. Still, Justice was special. Justice was *very* special!

For the past ten days, Justice had treated Baylee to dinner at one or the other of the various eating establishments in the Dickens Village. Sure, she was secretly disappointed that he hadn't asked her out on a real date—something other than their work lunch break. But still, ten days and ten dinners in the company of Justice Kincaid? It was fabulous! Furthermore, he'd stayed true to his word in making certain Candice didn't ever get stuck eating dinner in Tate's company again. In fact, after Candice enjoyed several evenings of dinner with different members of the security staff, Justice's friend Tristan revealed a bit of his possessive nature toward Candice and kindly told Justice to "butt out"—that he could "take it from here." Thus, Candice had begun to "really like" Tristan and had joined Baylee in hanging out on the mythical cloud nine the past few evenings.

"You know, you're a very thoughtful girl, Baylee Cabot," Justice said, tucking the card she'd given him into his coat pocket and returning his attention to the mug of hot chocolate sitting on the table before him.

"No," Baylee said, however. "I'm just sappy—and proud of it, by the way."

Justice was smiling at her when she looked at him again. "I think I already love you because of that too," he said.

This wasn't the first time Justice had teased her about loving her because of some part of her character or something she'd done. At first Baylee had found it flattering—sort of dreamily hopeful. But now, it kind of bothered her—made her wonder if he was the type of man that just tossed out the word *love* as casually as if it were the word *pickle*. But she decided not to be too suspicious or harsh in judging why Justice did it. She decided to enjoy it—the way she had the times before.

And so Baylee simply responded to his teasing the way she had every other time. "I hope so."

Justice chuckled and savored a few sips of hot

chocolate. Baylee smiled, liking the way his Adam's apple moved when he swallowed. Geez! Even his Adam's apple was handsome.

Unexpectedly he asked, "Are you going to that thing they're having tomorrow?"

Baylee tried to keep her heart from leaping in her chest with hope—hope that Justice was about to ask if she would go with him. He might simply be asking to make casual conversation. But her heart leapt anyway.

"You mean the tenth anniversary party for the Dickens Village thing?" she asked. After all, she wanted to make sure she'd understood what he was referring to.

"Yeah," he affirmed. "Are you going?"

"Well, we're not performing tomorrow night, so I thought I would at least drop in," she said. "I hear they're having the bakery cater part of it, after all… and you know what a sucker I am for good bread. How about you?"

Baylee held her breath. Was he planning on going? Would she get to see him there? Would he make her dreams come true and ask her to go with him?

Justice shrugged. "I was considering it."

Baylee tried to mask her disappointment—tried to find the courage to urge him to go.

But before she could begin to speak, he asked, "Wanna go with me?"

"Absolutely!" she answered—far too enthusiastically, as usual.

Justice smiled. "Good. And maybe they'll have lots of butter to spread on the bakery's bread goods."

"And maybe the bread will be warm and the butter will melt all over it! Mmmm!" Baylee giggled.

"You know, Baylee…you melt *my* butter sometimes, you little bell ringer," Justice said, winking at her flirtatiously.

Baylee giggled. "I melt your butter? Where'd you dig up that line, Casanova?"

"But you do," he assured her. "When I'm having dinner with you, I feel just like one of those bakery rolls—all fresh and slathered in butter…and then you warm me up and melt it."

Baylee laughed, rolling her eyes with simultaneous delight and amusement. "Oh my gosh! You are hysterical…*and* completely full of beans."

"I'm full of a lot more than beans," he chuckled. "But not when it comes to flirting with you, sugar plum."

"Sugar plum?" Baylee giggled. "And you're actually going to sit there and tell me you're not full of beans?"

"Wanna just leave right from here tomorrow?" he asked, purposefully changing the line of conversation. "If we just go straight there, we'll be there by seven. That's plenty of time, don't you think?"

"Yes, pony boy, it is," she answered.

"Pony boy?" Justice exclaimed with a grimace. "I choose sugar plum for you, and I get pony boy?"

"Hey!" Baylee teasingly scolded, wagging an index finger at him. "I'll have you know that before I fell in love with handbells, I loved ponies…and there was a little song my grandmother used to sing to me called

'Pony Boy.' So don't knock my nicknames."

"Oh, okay," Justice said, smiling. "Sorry. I just had a high school flashback there for a moment...and it wasn't a good one."

Baylee smiled with sudden insight. "Oh yeah... *The Outsiders*. Required reading...with that character named Ponyboy."

"Absolutely," Justice confirmed. "I hated that book. The ending sucked."

Baylee giggled, sipped her hot chocolate, and then said, "I'll think of something else then, okay?"

"Thanks," he sighed, winking at her. "So leaving right from work is okay with you tomorrow night?"

"Absolutely," she said—far too eagerly.

"All right then," he said, standing up from his chair. "I've got to get back now. So you have a wonderful rest of the evening, sugar plum...and I'll see you after work at nineteen hundred hours tomorrow night, okay?"

"Okay," Baylee giggled.

Justice winked at her once more, returned the tattered black top hat to his head, and hurried out the front door of the restaurant. It had been a quick exit, Baylee noted. And as she watched Justice jog across the square, looking as though he were talking to himself, she immediately realized that something must be up. Someone must have said something to him through the earpiece in his right ear that urged him to leave her so quickly after dinner—especially when there were still fifteen minutes left of their lunch hour.

Baylee frowned—for the realization caused a more

than slight anxiety to rise in her. Still, she figured it was probably something not too serious. After all, what could possibly happen in the Dickens Village?

❦

"DNA evidence confirms it," Brian said. "It's our Jack the Ripper copycat."

Justice frowned. The news was bad—worse than he'd hoped to hear.

"But this victim…she wasn't even a prostitute," Tristan noted aloud as he scanned the memo Brian handed him.

"Neither was the last victim," Brian said. "Our perp is changing his MO…becoming more desperate… spiraling."

"Two victims in two weeks…and this one was here in this city," Justice mumbled. "He will target the Dickens Village. It's obvious. Look where this victim lived."

"Exactly," Brian confirmed. "Two miles from the Dickens Village—that's where she lived. And the body was found a mile and half from the village. He's prowling—hunting. He's probably already been to the village more than once."

Justice thought about suggesting the FBI close the Dickens Village, but he knew that wouldn't fly. He knew the best way to catch the serial copycat killer was to bait him with the tempting lure of the Dickens Village. Naturally, the Dickens Village wasn't the killer's perfect vision of a hunting ground—being that it was 1840s era and the original Jack the Ripper terrorized London in the late 1880s and early 1890s. But for a copycat psycho killer, the Dickens Village was the closest he could come to living out his fantasy of being the true Ripper.

The photos of the copycat killer's seventh victim were gruesome. Justice had seen some gruesome stuff in his time, but something about the nature of what the killer did to the bodies of his victims sickened him. He began to perspire a bit, feeling more agitated than usual when working a case, and he knew why—Baylee.

"This victim worked at a clothing store?" he mumbled as his anxiety increased.

"Yep," Brian affirmed. "An upstanding young woman. There's no reason he should've targeted her. He's spiraling. The bureau is sure of it, and so am I."

"Kincaid and Holloway are worrying about their caroling handbell ringers just now," one of the men chuckled. "Wondering if the Ripper has seen them and—"

"Hey, Nichols," Justice interrupted, still studying the information Brian had handed him, "if I were you, I'd be worried about finding an IED shoved up your—"

"That's enough," Brian interrupted. "We need to tighten it from now on. Fifteen minute breaks only… and at the most. And I might have to have some of you pull some double shifts."

"Roger that," Justice mumbled.

"Let's keep the schedule as it is today," Brian continued. "Keep to your times…strictly to your times.

But tomorrow, let's double it up a bit…especially after eight p.m. Okay?"

Everyone agreed and, when Brian dismissed them, began to mill around and talk amongst themselves.

"I don't like this," Tristan said to Justice. "I thought it was a fluke when the bureau pegged the Dickens Village as a target for this scum."

"I know," Justin agreed. "So did I. And now he's changed his victim pattern. Any woman is at risk now. We better step it up and find this guy fast."

"And you had to go and get me all interested in Candice," Tristan said, jamming an elbow into Justice. "Damn! I've always dreaded the day when my job would impact my personal life. Thanks a lot, buddy."

"It always happens…sooner or later," Justice said, frowning as he looked to Tristan. "And you fell for Candice on your own, bra. I only introduced you. And besides, I'm in the stewpot with you, man. I don't like this at all." He looked back to the info sheet. "Brunette, early twenties, five foot five inches, a hundred and twenty pounds…dammit! This victim even had brown eyes. She fits Baylee's description to a tee, man!"

Tristan inhaled a deep breath—exhaled it slowly. "I hate this one, man," he growled. "And we'll just have to employ Eagle Eye on our shweeties. And that ain't a bad thing, after all, right?"

Justice grinned at Tristan as they bumped fists. "Nope. That ain't a bad thing at all."

"My shift starts in fifteen minutes, dude," Tristan

said as he stood up from his chair. "I'll see you at the shindig tonight, all right?"

"Absolutely," Justice assured him.

But even as he sat considering his and Tristan's plan to employ Eagle Eye (their method of keep a tight watch on any possible victim they considered to be prime), he didn't feel any calmer about the fact that Jack the Ripper was roaming the streets of the city looking for his next victim. He turned the page on the info sheet and exhaled a heavy sigh of trepidation. Especially when his last two had fit Baylee's basic description almost perfectly.

Justice ran his hand back over the top of his head through his short dark hair. He sighed once more, thinking that there were times he really hated his job—times when special ops missions in the Middle East didn't seem half as nerve-racking as chasing down some psychopathic killer whose victims matched the description of the girl he was planning on getting serious with.

❦

"Are you all right?" Baylee asked as she walked with Justice toward the Dickens Village main offices. He'd been frowning ever since she'd gotten out of her car in the parking lot to meet him.

He looked at her, and the frown puckering his movie-star brow softened as he grinned at her. "Yeah. Just a little tired," he answered.

But Baylee wasn't convinced that his frown had simply been borne of fatigue. She began to wonder if maybe he'd changed his mind about wanting her to go with him to the Dickens Village anniversary party.

Yet when his smile broadened and he said, "But now that I'm with you, I'm feeling my oats again," and laid one muscular arm across her shoulders, her worries about whether she were the cause of his frown dissipated.

"What exactly does that mean anyway?" she giggled, warmed by the feel of his body next to hers. "Feeling your oats? I've always wondered that. I mean…I know what sewing your oats means…but *feeling* your oats?"

"Ah! Finally," Justice said then, pulling her a little more snugly under his arm and against him. "At last I know something someone else doesn't. I've been waiting my whole life for this moment."

Baylee giggled. "Well, I'm glad I'm ignorant enough to oblige."

He chuckled and then began, "The term 'feeling my oats' or 'feeling your oats' or 'feeling his oats' or 'feeling her oats' or—"

"Okay…I get it already," she playfully sighed, jabbing an elbow in his side.

"The phrase actually finds its origins in horse racing," he explained. "A bucket of oats would be given to a racehorse on the day of, or just before, a race. The high-fiber carbs gave or give the horse a short burst of added energy."

"Like eating a candy bar in the middle of the afternoon makes you feel better for twenty minutes," Baylee noted.

"Absolutely," Justice confirmed. "So right now you're having the same effect on me that a bucket of oats before a race has on a racehorse."

Baylee shook her head with amusement. "Where do you come up with this stuff?" she giggled with delight. She loved the way he flirted—absolutely loved it!

"What stuff? I'm just telling it the way it is, that's all," he said as he opened the door to the Dickens Village office conference room.

As she preceded Justice into the conference room, a wave of awed delight washed over her—for everything before her was simply stunning! The large conference room had been decorated in the very same manner as the Dickens Village itself. Pine boughs, holly, pinecones, mistletoe, and so many miniature lights swathed the room at every wall, corner, table, and chair—it was simply enchanting! The warm aroma of fresh bread swirled through the room, mingled with the titillating scents of spices, sugars, chocolate, berries, and every other delicious smell.

Of course, nothing smelled as good as the fragrance of whatever brand and scent of deodorant, aftershave, or cologne that Justice was wearing. Baylee had committed the scent to memory the moment Justice had put his arm around her. It was a sporty, fresh sent, blended with the faint bouquet of soot, warm wool, and cool night breezes—and Baylee knew nothing would ever smell as good to her again as Justice Kincaid had the moment he'd put his arm around her.

"Mmmm!" Justice moaned, inhaling deeply. Glancing down at Baylee, he smiled and asked, "Do you smell that?"

Baylee giggled and nodded. "Bread and butter!"

"Absolutely!" he chuckled. "Come on, and let's eat something. I'm starving."

"Me too," Baylee said.

Justice dropped his arm from her shoulder and took her hand, leading her toward one of the tables so laden with food and beautiful greenery, decorations, and lights that Baylee wondered how it was even possible the table wasn't sagging in the middle.

Once Justice had piled two plates with good things to eat, he sought out a table for them, and they settled down.

Baylee grinned as she watched Justice dig into a huge slab of ham.

"What?" he asked, glancing up at her to see her amusement.

"Nothing," she replied. "I was just thinking what a pig you must think I am. Every time you see me, I'm eating."

"That's not true," he countered, however. "Sometimes you're singing, sometimes you're ringing your cute little bells, sometimes you're sitting at a table in that little cider place drinking cider with Candice... sometimes you're kneeing that Tate Polanski idiot in the chongs for touching you without your permission, and sometimes you're talking to that little kid who's always limping around with the crutch like he's Tiny Tim."

Baylee felt her mouth fall open a little with astonishment—stared at him with disbelief. He *had* been watching her from the rooftops of the Dickens Village! She was simultaneously elated and freaked out. She tried to think of how many times she'd adjusted her bra or stockings since she'd been performing at the Dickens Village. Had she done anything entirely embarrassing that he may have seen?

Yet to know he was watching her—that he was interested in her enough to keep such a close eye on her—it thrilled her!

"Wow…you're pretty observant," she said.

Justice paused in chewing a bite of ham, looked at her, and said, "Surveillance, Baylee…it's what I'm good at."

"Surveillance and seduction," she mumbled aloud to herself.

"What?" he asked.

"Nothing," she lied, pinching off a piece of a dinner roll and popping it in her mouth. "Mmm. I love this bread!"

In truth, Justice had heard exactly what Baylee had mumbled—that he was good at surveillance *and* seduction. He was pleased—more than pleased. For one thing, the flirting and attention he'd been casting at her seemed to be working a little. She liked it when he flirted with her; he could tell by the smiles and blushes that always leapt to her face. Furthermore, he figured if she found him somewhat seductive, then maybe his chances of reeling her in were better than he'd even hoped.

He did need to find a way to have her all to himself, however—alone—and outside the realm of the Dickens Village. Oh, dinner every night was all well and fine, but he needed to find out if she liked him when he wasn't dressed up like Dick Van Dyke and working. Moreover, he was ready—more than ready—ready to lay one on the little velvet-swathed bell ringer and see how she responded.

For a moment, the anxiety that wracks every teenage boy before kissing a girl washed over him—the fear of rejection, the fear that he might screw up the kiss and gross her out. But he reminded his stupid brain that he was a man now and far beyond that pimple-faced, awkward stage. Besides, it wasn't like it was his first time kissing a girl. What was there to screw up?

Still, as Justice watched Baylee butter another dinner roll, smiling as the butter began to melt, he frowned a little—annoyed at the little lingering doubt in himself that was still nagging him. Surely he could kiss her well enough to please her—couldn't he?

"So you're off tomorrow?" Baylee asked, rattling him from his flashback to adolescence.

"Oh…um…yeah," he managed. "It'll be my last day off for a while. We're stepping up security at the village, and we're all gonna be working some doubles."

The minute it was out of his mouth, Justice knew

he'd messed up. He watched Baylee's brow pucker with concern.

"Why?" she asked. "Why do you need to beef up security?"

Justice had lost his focus and revealed too much about the situation. To compound his frustration, the descriptions of the copycat killer's victims flooded his thoughts, reminding him how closely they all resembled his favorite little Victorian caroler.

He shrugged, feigning indifference, and lied, "O'Sullivan thinks shoplifting will increase the closer we get to the holidays." He hated lying to her, but he had his orders. Furthermore, he didn't want to raise any red flags in her brain that might prey on her sense of safety.

"Well, that stinks," she mumbled.

"And it gets worse," he added. "No more hour breaks for lunch or dinner."

"What?" she exclaimed—and Justice was inwardly pleased by her obvious distress. "I-I mean…you have to eat sometime, don't you?" she added, trying to make it appear that her concern was for the well-being of his appetite and not because they wouldn't be able to have dinner together every evening anymore.

In fact, the disappointment apparent in her pretty brown eyes was so obvious that, before he could think it over more thoroughly, he asked, "Are you off tomorrow too?" even though he knew she was. He'd kept a tight watch on her work schedule all week.

"Yeah," she answered. "Finally."

"Well, since we'll be working double-shifts and all for a while, I'm gonna do some early Christmas shopping tomorrow. If you don't have plans, would you be willing to help me out?"

Baylee was struck silent for a moment. Christmas shopping with Justice Kincaid? There wasn't anything in all the world she'd rather do on her day off. Suddenly she felt as warm as the melting butter on her dinner roll.

"I would love it!" she answered—way too enthusiastically, as usual.

"Good," he chuckled, obviously amused by her exuberance. "And if you've got things you need to check off your list…let's make a day of it. And maybe you'll let me take you out to for a *real* dinner date afterward, huh?"

You can take me anywhere anytime, you gorgeous chimney sweep, you, Baylee thought to herself. Out loud, however, she said, "That sounds wonderful! I'm in."

"Great," he said, cutting another piece of ham from the quickly disappearing slab on his plate. "Slather some butter on one of those rolls for me, will you, please?"

"Of course," Baylee giggled.

As she buttered a warm dinner roll for Justice, she sighed. Christmas shopping and dinner? Could it be real? Was it truly possible that Justice Kincaid was as interested in her as he seemed to be? And why would a guy like him be interested in a girl like her—a simple, regular, everyday girl who had no reason to catch the eye of a man with his background, experience, charm, and lethal good looks?

Still, inhaling a breath of determination to be confident and not look a gift horse in the mouth, so to speak, Baylee offered the freshly buttered dinner roll to Justice.

As Justice said, "Thank you," and accepted the roll from Baylee, she noticed that the butter on the roll had already begun to melt and had dribbled down the side of her hand. Reaching for a napkin with her free hand with which to wipe the melted butter, she was startled when Justice took hold of her wrist.

"Let me get that for you," he said.

Baylee felt her mouth drop open in rapturous awe as she watched, and felt, Justice Kincaid lick the butter dripping from the side of her hand. Goose bumps erupted over her body like a wave of stacked dominoes tripping.

He smiled at her, winked, and said, "I don't waste butter...ever."

"Oh," she managed to breathe, still overwhelmed with the sense of intoxication his gesture had rinsed her in.

Justice nodded toward her plate. "You better eat something besides bread, sugar plum," he urged. "Get a little protein into your system there."

"Oh...oh, yes," Baylee stammered, still so affected by his having licked the butter from her hand that she could hardly speak or move—or even think clearly.

Almost robotically she watched as her hands used her utensils to cut a bite of ham—as her fork lifted the piece to her mouth and inserted it. The familiar feeling of doubt, of wondering if she were really sitting at a table with Justice Kincaid, lingered all around her. Yet when he began telling her a few of the things he needed to pick up on their shopping excursion the next day, the truth of it all began to settle in. Though she didn't know why—though she couldn't fathom why Justice had chosen her to spend his time with—the fact of the matter was that he had! And as her senses began to return, Baylee decided that the old adage of looking a gift horse in the mouth finally made sense to her. It didn't matter why Justice was interested in getting to know her. All that mattered was that he was. So she wouldn't waste any more energy on doubt and wondering why the gift horse had been gifted. She'd simply accept it and ride away into the sunset as far as the horse could carry her.

CHAPTER SIX

Baylee and Justice mingled with friends and acquaintances, ate too many sweet treats, laughed and talked, and did everything else everyone attending the Dickens Village anniversary soiree did. Yet all the while Baylee was distracted—distracted by her feral attraction to the ferociously handsome Justice Kincaid—distracted by the schoolgirl's, dreamlike nature of her thoughts concerning him. She had visions of him all decked out in a tuxedo and watching her as she approached him wearing a bridal gown. She had visions of being held in his arms and gazing up into the mesmerizing peacock-green of his eyes. She wondered if he were a good kisser—then scolded herself for such a ridiculous thought. Of course he was a good kisser! How could he not be? She imagined that kissing Justice Kincaid would be the experience of a lifetime—of an eternity! Just thinking about kissing him caused her to blush—caused her body to warm all over and her mouth to water.

In truth, Baylee couldn't think of anyone or

anything in all her life to that point that made her feel the way she felt when she was in Justice's company—when she was simply looking at him from across the room. The thought entered her mind that she'd even toss her handbells into a melting pot if it meant she could win the affections and heart of Justice Kincaid.

How could she have such strong feelings for him already? she wondered as she sipped the last swig of hot chocolate from a mug Justice had handed her some time before. She'd only known him—what—less than two weeks? And yet she wanted him—she wanted him to be the mythical "Mr. Right" that every girl was always looking for—that she was always looking for. She wanted Justice to be her Mr. Right more than she'd ever wanted anything! But was it too much to hope for? She knew it was. And yet he did seem genuinely pleased to be in her company—to be with her, to talk with her, to drink hot chocolate with her.

Baylee watched Justice as he stood some distance away talking to Candice and Tristan. He was so handsome! Truly! He couldn't be real, could he? Surely he hadn't just glanced over at *her* and winked—not at *her*! But when she saw him say something to Tristan and then turn and begin striding toward her, Baylee smiled, forgot her doubts and wonderings, and simply enjoyed the rhythm of his ultra cool manner of walking—bathed in the pure perfect beauty of his handsome face and dazzling smile.

"Are you getting tired yet?" he asked as he reached her.

Baylee shook her head. "No. Not at all," she fibbed. And it was a lie, for in truth she was really, really tired. But she wasn't going to miss a moment in Justice's company—not for anything—especially something stupid like fatigue.

"Well, you're a better man than me then," he chuckled. "I'm beat. I'm probably just anticipating working double shifts, but I'm tired all the same. Do you mind if we cut out in a little while?"

"Not at all," she answered truthfully.

"I mean, I guess you can stay if you like…since you have your car here and everything," he offered.

But Baylee shook her head. "Nope. I've eaten enough to feed a small country already, and now that you've mentioned it…I guess I am feeling a little worn around the edges."

"Okay," he said, smiling at her. "We'll go in a few minutes then. I'll make sure you get to your car okay and then…"

He paused a moment as the soft classical music that had been wafting through the room a moment before changed. Baylee recognized the music—the song. It was one of her favorites. In fact, normally whenever she heard Joss Stone's rendition of "I Put a Spell on You," she couldn't help but sing along with the jazzy blues number. However, this time—considering she was in a room full of Dickens Village employees—she bit her tongue.

"Man, I love this song," Justice said. "Especially this Joss Stone version."

Baylee's mouth dropped open in elated astonishment. "You're kidding," she said. "Me too… but I've really never met anybody else who is at all familiar with this version."

Justice frowned. "Seriously? Joss Stone? She's awesome."

Baylee smiled as she noted the way Justice's body began to move in time to the music. It was barely perceivable, but very, very, *very* cool.

Oh, no, she thought—because it looked as if Justice Kincaid were about to wow her even more than he already had, with a smooth, cool manner of dancing. He moved with a perfectly marvelous rhythm that caused Baylee's heart to race and her mouth to water.

As people around them began splitting into couples to slow dance, Justice said, "Hmmm. I guess we're not the only Joss Stone fans in Dickens Town after all."

"I guess not," Baylee agreed. "Though I like this song no matter who's singing it most of the time."

"Me too," he said as he hands went to her waist and pulled her body toward his. "Wanna dance with me?" he asked.

Was he kidding? Was he blind? Was he for real? Of *course* she wanted to dance with him! Furthermore, she loved the way he'd begun dancing with her before he'd even asked her.

"Are you asking or telling?" she teased him.

Justice chuckled, his eyes narrowing with a far too seductive expression. "Whichever you prefer," he answered.

Baylee giggled. "Do you ever stop?" she asked.

"Stop what?" he asked in return.

"Stop with the charming, sort of provocative one-liners."

He smiled at her—slowly slid his hands up her sides to the underside of her arms and then over the underside of her arms, lifting them and gently gripping her wrists a moment as he settled her hands on his shoulders.

Wrapping his arms around her body and pulling her against him, he mumbled, "Nope."

Baylee, now breathless in his embrace, whispered, "Oh, good."

As the song continued, Baylee wished someone would just hit the repeat button so that it would never end. Just as she'd suspected, being held by Justice Kincaid was the most euphoric sensation a woman could experience. She could feel the heat of his body, the solid, muscular contours of it—even for their costumes. She consciously felt safer—more protected than she ever had in her entire life. Likewise, she was aware of the potent desires welling in her—the desire to caress his whiskery, soot-smeared fact with her hands, the desire to kiss him, to feel his mouth pressed to hers.

I think I already love you, Justice's voice echoed in her mind.

I know I already love you, her own thoughts answered.

Everything, every sensation and romantic thought in her, became more powerful when Justice lowered his head to press his cheek against hers—began to mumble into her ear words similar to those Joss Stone was singing. "I'd put spell on *you* if I could," he breathed. The warmth of his breath on her neck—the heat of his skin next to hers—sent a rush of goose bumps surging over her body. "I'd put a spell on you and make you mine."

Baylee trembled a little—overcome with desire, hope, and disbelief. Surely he just didn't know the lyrics as well as she did. After all, it wasn't like Justice would really want her to be his.

"I thought you liked this song," she baited him, desperately hopeful that she was wrong—that he really did know the lyrics as well as she did and had intentionally changed them for her sake.

"I do," he said, raising his head to look at her. "Why?"

She was at his mercy—utterly at his mercy! As she gazed up into Justice's ridiculously handsome face, she ventured, "Well, the words to the song are actually—"

"I know the words to the song, Baylee," he said, grinning at her. "And I think you know that, don't you?"

She thought she might cry—burst into tears of perfect happiness! "M-maybe," she stammered, trying to keep tears from welling in her eyes.

Justice chuckled. "Maybe?" He laughed, amused by her response. His arms tightened around her then, and he rested his chin on her head a moment. "Maybe." He laughed again, and Baylee sighed—swept away in the blissful sound of his voice rumbling in his broad chest.

The song was nearing the end, and Baylee frowned. Their dance was almost over. She couldn't keep her body from reacting to the truth of it, and her arms rather involuntarily slid over his shoulders, her hands lacing at the back of his neck. She didn't want him to release her—ever!

But the song did end, and people at the party began talking and returning to the food tables as another, more upbeat selection started. Baylee felt herself blush with the realization that she was still clinging to Justice, even after the music had stopped. Unwillingly, but quickly, she released him as his embrace of her slackened.

"Do you want something to drink before we go?" Justice asked as he released Baylee altogether—leaving her feeling cold, nervous, and saddened.

"No…I'm okay," she answered.

"Good job, man!" another security guard dressed as a chimney sweep said, patting Justice on one strong shoulder. "You're slick, Kincaid. Real slick!"

"Thanks, man," Justice said, nodding at the man.

"I guess you've got more than just weapons expertise, huh?" the guy asked. "You're a tactical master too."

"You bet," Justice chuckled.

Baylee frowned with puzzlement as the guy smiled at her. "What?" she asked. "Am I missing something?"

Justice grinned, his grin slowly spreading into a full-fledged smile. "I've been waiting for a chance like this for quite a while now," he said.

"A chance like what?" she giggled.

"Mistletoe, shweety," the other chimney sweep said.

"What?" But when Bailey looked up to see she stood directly beneath a large mistletoe ball hanging from an overhead light, she understood.

Smiling with profound pleasure, she looked back to Justice. "Did you maneuver me here on purpose?"

"Of course," he answered. "Maneuvers, Baylee... it's what I'm good at."

She giggled and then gasped, breathless with anticipation, as Justice reached out, taking her face between his warm, powerful hands. "Come here, you little bell-ringer, you," he said in a low, provocative voice. "Let's see if I can ring your bell for a change, shall we?"

Baylee gulped. Would he really kiss her? And if he did, would he kiss her on the cheek or the...

Justice's kiss was confident and solidly applied. There was no timid, tender, practical kiss to Baylee's lips, but he didn't kiss her too forcefully either. He simply kissed her—and yet there was nothing whatsoever simple about it! In fact, it was the most perfect kiss Baylee could have ever dreamt of. Justice's lips weren't closed tight when he kissed her, but neither was his mouth wide open and excessively aggressive. His lips were parted, moist, and warm when they first met hers, and the feel of it all sent wave after wave of tingling, thrilling goose bumps streaming over Baylee's body. And yet, as if he knew she had been unprepared for such a perfect kiss the first time around, Justice kissed her again—allowing Baylee the opportunity to part her lips enough so that her returned kiss matched his as perfectly as if their mouths were made to be melded. Leaning forward so that his strong body was flush with her own, Justice kissed her a third and wildly exciting time. Three kisses—only three—and neither of the three lasting beyond a few seconds—and yet Baylee Cabot wanted nothing more than to throw her arms around Justice's neck and continuing kissing him for the rest of her life!

Baylee felt her eyes flutter open as their third kiss ended, not even having realized she'd closed them. She was suddenly aware of the catcalls echoing through the room and felt herself blush as she gazed up into the oh-so-breathlessly handsome, soot-smudged face of Justice Kincaid. His peacock-green eyes smoldered with a modest satisfaction in the low lighting. He grinned as Baylee attempted to appear unruffled.

"Well?" he asked.

"W-well, what?" Baylee stammered in a breathless whisper.

"Did my pathetic attempt to ring the little bell-ringer's bell...did it work?" he chuckled.

But Baylee couldn't verbally respond. She could only endure the deepening of the already rose-red blush on her cheeks.

"She looks like she's thinking 'ding-ding-ding' to me, Justice," Tristan chuckled as he approached. He reached out and playfully pinched Baylee's cheek as Justice released her. "Now *that's* the way it's done, people!" Tristan laughed. "Never let a good sprig of mistletoe go to waste." Tristan winked at Baylee, and she felt somewhat forgiving of his teasing.

"Come on," Justice said, taking Baylee's arm. "I'll walk you to your car."

"You don't have to do that," Baylee began to argue.

But Justice shook his head. "It's cold, late, and dark. What kind of a man would I be if I let a shweet little bell-ringer like you walk out to the parking lot all alone?"

"But…" she began to argue again. She was so dazed by the lingering bliss kissing him had caused that she couldn't even think straight at first.

But when he asked, "Are you gonna let me be a gentleman or not, sugar plum?" she remembered that they had come to the party together, so it only made sense they should leave together.

"I-I guess I'm just not used to there being any gentlemen around," she stammered, trying to mask how thoroughly discombobulated she was.

"Well, that's just wrong," he sighed. Placing one strong arm across her shoulders, he pulled her against him to tuck her securely under his arm.

Baylee didn't know how she managed to walk to the door with him. In fact, she wondered if she'd simply floated there with the help of the proverbial cloud nine.

As they exited the building Justice said, "Brrrr! It's cold out here."

But Baylee didn't think it was cold. In fact, she couldn't remember a time in her life when she'd been as warm as she was at that moment. She loved the feel of his arm around her—of his holding her protectively as they walked across the parking lot.

Again Baylee could smell the comforting aroma of the bakery wood smoke still clinging to Justice's chimney sweep jacket, of the soot on his clothes and face, and of the faint scent of his unidentified, masculine antiperspirant. Oooo! Justice Kincaid smelled *so* good!

"Do you girls wear long underwear under these dresses?" he asked, shivering again. "I hope you do, because I'm sure it's just going to get colder and colder as the season progresses."

"I'm warm enough," she answered. "But how about you?"

"I'm fine," he said. "Just being kind of a baby tonight because it was so warm inside, I guess. I'm not really a fan of really cold weather."

"But cold weather is the best way to be cozy," Baylee offered. "Evenings in front of the fire, drinking hot chocolate, and watching Christmas shows on TV aren't nearly as cozy and wonderful in the summertime."

He chuckled. "Good point...though I admit to not spending a whole lot of time watching Christmas shows on TV."

Baylee shrugged. "Actually, I don't either...but I wish I could."

"I like your little red car," he chuckled as they walked toward Baylee's Honda.

"Me too," she agreed. "It gets me where I need to go, and it's never let me down yet."

"Between your car and your cute little caroler dress…you're about as festive as they come," he teased.

"I try," Baylee giggled.

Reaching into the deep pocket of her red velvet caroler's cape, Baylee fumbled around for her keys.

"Thanks for walking me out," she said as she continued to fumble.

As she pulled the keys from her pocket at last, Justice said, "Thanks for letting me kiss you under the mistletoe back there."

Baylee blushed. "Well, I can just imagine what it must be like—you know, all your chimney sweep, Special Forces friends standing around and—"

"That's not why I did it," he interrupted. She looked up to see him staring at her with a somewhat perturbed expression on his face. "I've never kissed a girl I didn't want to kiss."

"Really?" she asked, more out of habit than doubt.

"Yeah, really," he affirmed. "I knew exactly where that mistletoe was in conjunction with your position in the room. Strategy, Baylee…it's what I'm…"

"It's what your good at, I know," Baylee giggled.

He nodded—chuckled at her wit. She gasped a little then as, in the next moment, he used his body to gently push hers back against her car.

Taking her face in his hands again, he mumbled, "And just to make sure you do…" the moment before he kissed her.

Again his kiss was confident without being too aggressive—just as it had been before. This time, however, it lingered. His mouth lingered against hers, warm and moist. Yet his manner of kissing her nearly frustrated her somehow, for it felt as if he were intentionally holding back, keeping a more passionate kiss in reserve. Her spinning senses managed to figure that he was probably being careful—not wanting her to think he was some kind of a creep who was out for only one thing. Yet she wanted him to kiss her more deeply—more passionately—but he didn't.

Oh, it was absolutely true that Justice's kisses were the stuff of dreams—would be the winner of any MTV Best Kiss Award! Still, Baylee knew there was more, that what she was experiencing was the literal tip of the iceberg—that if he ever wanted to kiss her with no restraint, she would never recover from the ecstasy of it!

"Good night, Baylee," he said as he released her and stepped back. "I'll see you tomorrow. Ten a.m., okay?"

"Of course," she answered, far too breathlessly. "Let me give you my address."

But Justice shook his head. "No need. Reconnaissance, Baylee…"

"It's what you're good at," she finished for him with a giggle.

"Among other things," he said insinuatively, with a wink.

Baylee's insides were boiling with the warm, summer butterflies of delight.

Taking her keys, he opened her door for her, returning them once she'd slid into the driver's seat.

"Good night," he said.

"Good night," she said as he closed her door.

Her hand was trembling as she put the key in the ignition and turned it. Glancing at Justice once more, she smiled before pulling away.

As Baylee drove home through the dark November night, she sighed. She was emotionally compromised—too goofy-minded with the residual euphoria of kissing Justice to be a safe driver. She wondered if what she was feeling were similar to what intoxicated people felt just before they called a cab to drive them home. And when she glanced in her rearview mirror to see that her nose, cheeks, and the skin around her mouth were smudged with soot—a transference from Justice's chimney sweep's face to hers that had occurred when they'd kissed—she nearly ran a stop sign as she'd giggled with delight.

Shaking her head and attempting to capture her wits once more, Baylee drove on—smiling as the warm sense of Justice Kincaid's kissing lingered on her lips.

CHAPTER SEVEN

Christmas shopping with Justice was nothing if not an adventure. Baylee was awed by the consideration and time he'd put into making his list. Furthermore, he certainly wasn't a cheapskate or skinflint. Though Justice may have dressed like a Dickens-era chimney sweep to blend into the Dickens Village atmosphere at work, there was nothing Scrooge-ish about him. And that fact alone would've made the experience fun for Baylee. Shopping with a man who'd set his Christmas budget realistically high and considered the gifts he'd wanted to give before December 22? It was wonderful!

However, it wasn't the time in the jewelry store searching for the perfect set of opal earrings he wanted for his mother or in the sporting goods store as he chose just the right trench knife for his younger brother that was the most fun. It was the sheer fact that she was with him at all that caused Baylee's heart to beat double time.

Not only was Justice generous, but it was obvious he truly enjoyed giving to those he loved. Baylee's admiration of Justice only continued to grow as the day proceeded. He was adorable to watch—the way his handsome face would light up when he'd found exactly what he'd been looking for. Selfishly, and without any right to do so, Baylee secretly wondered what Justice would choose to give her, if she were someone fortunate enough to be cherished by him and therefore found her name on his Christmas gift-giving list. Of course, he didn't know her very well, she reminded herself. But still, she wondered what he'd give her—if the occasion ever presented itself for him to give her something.

Once they had grabbed a quick lunch at a sandwich shop, they were in Justice's truck and off and running once more.

"Now, Grandma is just about the hardest one on my list," he said as he drove them toward the high-end strip mall on the east side of town.

"Why don't you just buy her a new car and give her the payment along with it?" Baylee teased.

Justice laughed. "That would be funny, right?" he began. "I could buy her, like, a new Shelby Mustang or something and wrap up the payment book and put it under the tree." He shook his head. "You don't know what a little pill my grandma can be. But she's one of those ladies that you can't help but love…no matter what kind of crap she pulls."

Baylee smiled, warmly delighted by Justice's obvious affection for his grandmother. "So what *are* you planning on getting for her?" she asked.

Justice paused a moment. "Well, if you really

want to know...this little subcompact Beretta nine-millimeter she's been hinting for all year," he answered.

Baylee frowned. "Um...a Beretta? As in a handgun?" She was astonished. Justice was planning on purchasing a handgun for his grandmother as a Christmas gift?

"Well, the one she carries now is just so heavy. And the Beretta Px4 Storm Subcompact pistol really is the best subcompact sidearm right now...in my opinion, anyway," he explained. "She's been carrying this big ol' Magnum for a couple of years, and though grandmas always seem to lug around heavy purses, I know the little Beretta will ease up her purse load a bit. So I had this gun shop order one in for me, and we just have to pick it up."

But Baylee giggled as she studied Justice for a moment as he drove. "You're serious, aren't you?"

"Absolutely," he assured her, glancing at her with not one hint of teasing in his eyes. "Grandma loves guns. She always has. She and Grandpa...well, let's just say they had—and she still has—quite an arsenal."

"Wow!" Baylee sighed. "It kind of makes me want to meet this Calamity Jane grandma of yours."

"Oh, you'll love her," he assured her—as if he fully expected her to meet his grandmother one day. "Like I said, she can be a handful, but she's hysterical at the same time. That's how she gets away with all the stuff she pulls on everybody."

Baylee kept smiling—sighed as she gazed out the truck window as they drove. It was wonderful, being with Justice. Absolutely wonderful! She wished the day would never end, but she knew it eventually would. Still, she hoped it would end with a good-bye kiss. She thought she'd do just about anything to experience another Justice Kincaid kiss.

"So I figure we'll do the gun store, then pick up that stuff at the mall you needed, and then..." He paused, looking over to her with a rather mischievous grin. "You know how I told you I'd take you out for a real dinner tonight?"

"Yeah?" she prodded as a warm, delightful sensation pressed the back of her neck.

"How about this? I set the DVR to record one of those girlie Christmas movies you chicks like so well last night. So how about I take you *in* for a real dinner instead, and we can watch a corny Christmas show while we eat? What do you say? I mean, we were talking about how we never get to watch stuff like that, right?"

"Absolutely," Baylee giggled. How adorable! How incredibly creative and thoughtful he was! She couldn't believe it. Surely it was just another thing about Justice that was too good to be true—wasn't it? Yet so far, everything that appeared too good to be true about him *was* true!

"Cool!" he said, smiling. "Then I hope you like French toast. It's what I'm good at," he said.

"French toast and seduction," Baylee mumbled to herself.

"What?" Justice asked.

"I said French toast...I love it," she answered.

"Oh, good," Justice said—though once again he'd heard exactly what Baylee had really said.

He smiled, proud of himself for having thought of the idea to take her *in* for dinner instead of out. He wanted this girl—wanted her to like him as much as he liked her—and if Brian was stepping up their shifts in order to better track the Jack the Ripper psycho, then Justice knew he needed to use the small windows of time he could grab with Baylee to the best advantage he could. Quality more than quantity—that's what he had to do. And he hoped a nice warm dinner of his special French toast, a corny, made-for-TV Christmas movie, and the opportunity to just spend more time with her would help his cause.

Yep. He had plans for the little handbell ringer sitting in the passenger's seat of his truck. But when the reality of why he and the others were posing as chimney sweeps at the Dickens Village in the first place polluted his thoughts, he wondered how he was going to stay on top of protecting all of humanity from a murderous and evil entity and still find time to woo and win Baylee Cabot.

❦

The exquisite dinner of French toast and bacon Justice had whipped up at his house after they'd finished shopping had been sublime—mostly because Justice had cooked it, of course, but it had been delicious all the same. Still, nothing would ever be more blissful for Baylee than the hour she'd spent since, sitting next to Justice on his couch, watching *Miracle of the Mistletoe*—the corny, yet very romantic, made-for-TV movie he'd recorded the night before. An hour into the movie and Baylee was having a hard time keeping track of the simplistic plot of the show—for in that sweet, romantic hour, Justice had often put his arm around her shoulders, rested a hand on her knee, or fiddled with the ring on her right ring finger. It was heaven being there with Justice—pure heaven.

It's why Baylee frowned when there was a knock on Justice's front door. It interrupted not only their movie but Baylee's being tucked warm and cozy under Justice's arm—against him.

"Who can that be?" he mumbled as he pressed the pause button on the remote control. He glanced at his wristwatch and frowned as he released Baylee and stood up from the couch. "Hold on a second, okay?"

"Of course," Baylee answered. Of course she'd hold on a second. She'd hold on for hours and hours if it meant she'd have the chance to cuddle up next to Justice for a while longer.

From her seat on Justice's leather couch, Baylee watched as Justice opened the front door—a broad smile spreading over his handsome face.

"What are you doing here?" he asked, still smiling.

"I came over to make sure you were all right, honey," a woman's voice said. The voice sounded like music, and as the elderly white-haired lady stepped over the threshold and into Justice's embrace, Baylee understood why.

She knew at once that this must be Justice's grandmother—the one that wanted a Beretta for Christmas.

"I'm fine, Grandma," Justice said. "I was just—"

"Ahhh!" the older woman said as she glanced over, catching sight of Baylee. "You were just necking, eh?"

"No, Grandma. I wasn't necking," Justice chuckled, closing the door behind his grandmother. "This is Baylee," he said, gesturing toward Baylee. "She and I were out all day Christmas shopping and thought we'd watch some TV and—"

"Neck?" the woman finished for him. "So what you meant was you're not necking *yet*."

The woman's eyes—her peacock-green eyes— were intent on Baylee as Baylee rose from her seat and walked over to meet her.

"I'm Baylee Cabot," Baylee said, offering a hand to the woman.

The woman's smile broadened. "And I'm Francis Kincaid," she said, taking Baylee's hand, "Justice's grandmother."

"It's so nice to meet you, Mrs. Kincaid," Baylee said, noting the way the woman clung to her hand. Mrs. Kincaid's hand was warm and soft—just as a grandmother's hand should be.

"So you've been necking with Justice, is that it, honey?" Mrs. Kincaid asked.

Baylee couldn't help blushing—not because she had been necking with Justice but because she *wished* she had been.

"Come on, Grandma," Justice scolded. "You'll scare her off. Do you know how long it took me to lure her here? Now what did you need?"

"Like I said, sweetie," Mrs. Kincaid answered, though her attention never left Baylee, "I just wanted to make sure you were all right...since I hadn't heard from you today."

"Well, I'm fine," Justice said. "And now you know it, and you can go home and...and do whatever you were doing before."

Mrs. Kincaid smiled, leaned closer to Baylee, and whispered, "He wants me out of the way so he can neck with you."

Baylee giggled. "I hope so," she jested in return—though she wasn't really in jest at all.

"Come on, Grandma," Justice said, taking his grandmother's arm in an attempt to lead her toward the door. "Do the cops know you're out driving the streets this late? They oughta issue a warning."

"Oh, you hush, Justice," she scolded. "My driving is fine, and you know it." Aside to Baylee, she added, "He worries just because of my age, you know. But I'm only seventy-two years old. I've got at least twenty years of good driving ahead of me, right?"

Baylee smiled and nodded.

"Grandma," Justice urged.

"Have you seen his muscles, honey?" Mrs. Kincaid asked, however. When Baylee didn't answer right away—too stunned by the question to have a rational response come to mind—Mrs. Kincaid added, "Have you?"

"Um…I don't think I have," Baylee managed to stammer.

Then Mrs. Kincaid looked to Justice, put her hands on her hips in a scolding manner, and asked, "How do you ever expect to get to necking with this young woman if she hasn't seen your muscles, Justice?"

"Grandma…it's time to go," Justice said patiently.

But Mrs. Kincaid wasn't having any of it. "Take that sweater off, Justice. Right now."

Justice was wearing a red ribbed shirt. It was long-sleeved and tight-fitting and had made Baylee's head swim with admiration when he'd first picked her up that day.

"It's not a sweater, Grandma, and you need to be on your way," Justice countered.

"Take it off this minute and show that girl your muscles!" Mrs. Kincaid demanded, stomping one foot on the floor.

"She doesn't want to see my muscles, Grandma," Justice argued. Baylee could see his patience was wearing thin—yet the entire scene was so amusing that she couldn't help but giggle.

"Of course she does!" Mrs. Kincaid argued. Looking to Baylee, she asked, "Don't you, honey?"

"Of course I do," Baylee answered, joining ranks with the older woman. The expression of astonishment on Justice's face was wildly entertaining—an expression of disbelief and, for the first time since she'd met him, dumbfoundedness.

"See there, Justice," Mrs. Kincaid said. "She *does* want to see your muscles. I don't know how you ever expect her to start necking with you if she doesn't see how pretty you are." Taking hold of the bottom of Justice's shirt then, Mrs. Kincaid endeavored to strip it off him.

"Knock it off, Grandma!" Justice growled. "That's enough."

Baylee watched then as Justice pulled his shirt back down over his stomach—but not before she caught a glimpse of the sculpted washboard abs he owned.

"Take it off," Mrs. Kincaid ordered, attempting to remove his shirt a second time.

"Leave it alone," Justice told her.

"Just for a minute, Justice," Mrs. Kincaid argued. "Give that girl a show, and she'll do anything you want her to do." She looked to Baylee again and asked, "Isn't that right, honey?"

"Absolutely," Baylee giggled, entirely amused by what was going on between Justice and his grandmother.

What she didn't expect, however, was for Justice to daringly arch one eyebrow as he looked at Baylee and asked, "Is that so?"

"Of course it's so," Mrs. Kincaid answered for her.

Justice smiled then, and the warm sensation that rose to the back of Baylee's neck every time he did so returned with a fury.

"Be careful what you promise, sugar plum," he said. "Someone might just call you on it one day."

And without another word, Justice reached over one shoulder, taking hold of the back of his shirt and stripping it off right there, in front of the leftover French toast and everything.

Though Baylee's mouth dropped open and she began to blush at the sight of Adonis in the living flesh, Justice's grandmother clapped her hands and laughed.

"See?" she squealed. "I told you his muscles were something, didn't I?"

In truth, Baylee was astonished—thoroughly intimidated by the sight of Justice shirtless. He was as ripped as any guy to ever star in a workout video infomercial, and all Baylee could do was stand there in front of Justice and his grandmother and blush to the marrow of her bones.

"Okay, Grandma…now go home," Justice told his grandmother as he opened the front door once more, took hold of her arm, and pulled her over the threshold.

"All right, all right," Mrs. Kincaid whined. "I'm going." But a moment before Justice closed the door in her face, she looked at Baylee and added, "I'm sure he's as good at necking as he looks too!"

"Good night, Grandma," Justice said, closing the door. Raising his voice so that his grandmother could hear him through it, however, he added, "Text me when you're home safe, okay?"

"Okay!" Baylee heard Mrs. Kincaid call from the other side.

Baylee watched as Justice peered through a slit in the blinds at the window next to his front door. "I always worry when she's driving at night. I'm sure she can't see as well in dim conditions as she professes." Justice seemed intent on watching his grandmother to her car, but when Baylee heard the roar of an engine, he sighed and stepped back from the blinds.

"Sorry about that," he said, smiling at her. "But I told you she was a pill."

"Yes, you did," Baylee admitted.

"Here," he said, tossing the waded-up red shirt Baylee had loved on him behind the couch. "This is all stretched out now. Let me go get something else. Hang on, okay?"

Baylee wanted to say, *You don't have to put on a shirt on my account*—but instead she simply said, "Absolutely."

Justice wasn't gone long, and when he returned, he had a folded red T-shirt in hand. "I will say this," he said as he held the T-shirt by the shoulders, shaking it out. "That was the fastest I've ever seen Grandma leave any place." He chuckled. "She thinks I'm going to be making out with you all night and is so desperate to see me settled down and happy that she was willing to hightail it."

Baylee giggled, and Justice paused in putting on the T-shirt. "What?" he asked.

"Necking," she giggled again. "It's just such a funny term."

"I know," Justice agreed. "It brings to mind visions

of people rubbing their necks together like giraffes or something."

"Yeah," Baylee laughed as she watched Justice put on the T-shirt. His torso had been bare long enough, however, for Baylee to notice not only the rippling muscles Justice owned but also several severe scars. There was one at his left shoulder—a brutal scar that looked to be left from some sort of intensive shoulder surgery. There were also several scars along his ribcage on the left side of his body, almost as if there were one for each rib. It was all she had time to notice, but it was enough to make her ponder a little more on what he'd said the night he'd told her she'd never seen him naked. His body was marked by the injuries he'd sustained during the helicopter crash and ensuing IED explosion. The scars she'd so briefly seen must've been what he'd been referencing that night.

"But she's off on her way now, so we can finish our epic movie," he said, smiling. "I'm riveted. I've just got to see how this all works out."

"Now don't be sarcastic," Baylee scolded as he sat down on the couch, took her hand, and pulled her to sit next to him. "It's a cute little holiday movie."

"I wasn't being sarcastic," he said, slipping an arm across her shoulders and picking up the remote. "But if Bianca doesn't end up with Paul, I'll be ticked off."

Baylee giggled and more than willingly cuddled up to him as he pulled her close.

"Ready?" he asked.

"Yeah," she answered.

As the movie resumed, Baylee wondered how a man could endure all that Justice had obviously endured during his time in the military and then just settle down on the couch and watch a corny Christmas movie. But then again, what else was a person supposed to do? She felt saddened—disturbed by the excruciating pain she knew he must've endured. And yet he seemed healthy and happy now. She'd just concentrate on the Justice Kincaid of now and not let her heart break by nesting on thoughts of him as a wounded soldier.

He chuckled a moment, and Baylee looked up at him. "What?" she asked, wondering if she'd missed something in the movie.

"Necking," he mumbled, however. "It is a weird thing to call it, isn't it?"

"Yeah," Baylee agreed, though she thought she'd love to be *necking* with Justice Kincaid just then. She quivered with delight at the mere thought of it, and Justice pulled her more tightly against him. He was so warm! It was intoxicating, the feel of him holding her.

And so, euphoric with the Justice-intoxication, Baylee sighed with contentment and pleasure and tried to focus on the comedic drama playing out on the TV.

❦

"That's it?" Justice exclaimed with disappointment. "That's how they're going to end this stupid movie?"

Baylee giggled. "What? You don't like happy endings?" she teased.

"Of course I like happy endings," he grumbled. He

clicked the off button on the TV remote. "But you call that a happy ending?"

"Well, they both discovered they loved each other…and managed to leave their significant others at the altar and race into each other's arms in the middle of New York City and kiss. What more do you want?"

"Kiss?" he asked, a grimace of disgust puckering his brow. He picked up a smaller remote that was lying on the floor, pointed it toward the iPod dock on his wall unit, and pushed a button. Music began to waft from the dock at a low volume, and Justice said, "We waited an hour and a half for that pathetic little peck at the end?"

"Well, at least he kissed her on the lips," Baylee pointed out, giggling with amusement at his obvious disapproval of the final kiss of the movie.

Justice rolled his eyes, however. "That was pathetic. I can't believe you women are content with a movie like that. Where's the romance? Where's the passion? Where's the good kissing? I thought you girls were all about good kissing."

"Well…it is what it is," Baylee said, shrugging. "What do you want me to do about it?"

The moment she looked at Justice, however, Baylee somehow knew exactly what he wanted her to do about it. Even before he said "satisfy me" and gathered her in his arms, she knew.

"I'm feeling dissatisfied, so satisfy me. That was the most pathetic movie kiss I've ever seen," he said, brushing a strand of hair from her face. "How about I show you how it should've ended, all right?"

Baylee couldn't speak. She could only gaze up at him—somehow hypnotized by the gorgeous peacock-green eyes that had been haunting her dreams every night for almost two weeks. She could only gaze up at him and nod.

"Now this, Baylee Cabot...you little bell-ringer, you...this is how it should've ended," he mumbled as his mouth pressed to hers. "Maybe a soft one like that at first," he whispered. "But then..." In one smooth motion, he left his seat on the couch, pulling her up to stand with him and wrapping her in his arms. "Then it should've gone more like this."

Driven, commanding—hot, moist, and intimate—that's what his next kiss was. It was mind-blowing and sent such a wave of heat and desire coursing through her body that she truly thought she might faint! But the kiss was too short, and she recovered fairly quickly. Too short it may have been, but it was life-altering all the same.

"See?" he said, still holding her against him. "*That's* how it should've ended."

Baylee swallowed the desire that was only expanding in her throat and said, "I see what you mean."

And then the music changed on the iPod dock. Baylee felt goose bumps racing over her arms and legs as she recognized the Jeff Beck guitar intro.

"Hey," Justice said, pulling her more snugly against him instead of releasing her. "It's our song."

"Our s-song?" Baylee stammered. It was hitting her full force then—the fact that she'd fallen irrevocably in love with Justice in the tight span and space of a mere eleven days.

"Yeah," he said, smiling down at her. "Remember last night at the party?"

Did she remember last night at the party? Was he kidding? Of course she remembered it.

"Of course," she breathed.

"Yeah…well, it's our song," he told her as if it were something everyone in the entire world knew except her. He smiled at her then, and his deep-green eyes began to smolder with such an expression of intent to seduce that it frightened Baylee a little. Furthermore, she couldn't believe what he asked her next.

"You wanna *neck* with me while it's playing?" he asked. "Just for my grandma's sake?" When she didn't answer—for she figured he'd probably read the "yes" in her eyes—he began to slow dance with her just a little, singing "I Put a Spell on You" with Joss Stone and wooing her into submission.

Baylee began to wonder if maybe Justice really did own some sort of strange power of bewitchment, for she truly felt as if she were under a sort of fairy tale enchantment, spell, or charm. In truth, Justice's natural charm—the powerful charisma and irresistible allure that literally oozed from every inch of his being—was enough to beguile her on its own. But add to it the way his deep voice provocatively sang the song to her as they swayed to the music—as his hands at her waist directed her as effectively as the slightest tug of the reins at a horse's bit directed it—and Baylee was no longer entirely convinced that there wasn't something supernatural about Justice Kincaid.

As he continued to provocatively sing about putting a "spell on you," Baylee felt herself begin to relax against him. His gaze held hers with such a mesmerizing grip that she could not look away from him. Moreover, she felt her own hands at his chest begin to slide upward to his shoulders, then around to the back of his neck. She trembled, still hypnotized by the simmering invitation in his peacock-green eyes, yet so powerfully overcome, with not only the physical desire to taste his kiss again but the nearly painful swelling of something akin to recognition in her heart, that she nearly quit breathing.

And then, without any further notice, Justice wrapped his arms around her, binding her against him as his mouth pressed firmly and confidently to hers, drawing her into joining him in a long, slow, rhythmic kiss. Baylee's knees began to buckle, but Justice held her unyieldingly, and she stiffened her stance, her hands softly caressing the back of his neck and head. Goose bumps broke over her body as the feel of his short hair tickled her palms. She quivered as his mouth ground against hers, demanding reciprocation—which she all too willingly gave.

As Joss Stone's raspy blues voice continued to weave a spell of heated desire throughout the room, Justice Kincaid continued to cast his own bewitching charm over Baylee. She was in trouble! She was entirely in trouble! She felt tears springing to her eyes, for the feel of his kiss melded to hers, of the moisture and flavor of their blended mouths, affirmed everything to her— that she wanted him—that she wanted Justice Kincaid to be her Mr. Right!

Wild, spontaneous thoughts began to crash around in her head—the thought that she'd give anything to be with him—that she'd give *up* anything to be with him. In that moment, she didn't care about her place in the Hampton Handbell Ringers. She didn't care about money or making a living. She didn't even care if she ever saw another loved one again in all her life! All she wanted was to be with Justice—to love him and win his love for her own somehow.

The crazy thoughts ripping through her only heightened Baylee's desire, and she kissed Justice hard, aggressively, and for a long, long time in response to his coaxing kisses. She loved him. She truly did love him! Baylee was so in love with Justice it hurt—caused her heart to feel as if it were tearing in two. She loved him, not just because he was the most handsome, physically attractive, and desirable man she'd ever seen in all her life but because her soul seemed to recognize his. She loved him. She loved him!

Justice could not satisfy his craving for her. No matter how hard he kissed Baylee, he still wanted more! The thirst he had for her mouth was insane. The thirst he had for *her* was insane!

Had he lost his mind? he wondered. A man couldn't really fall in love with a woman over the course of just a few days, could he? But he knew he had. In fact, he'd known he would nearly from the moment he'd first set eyes on her after the orientation at the Dickens Village offices. He'd known he wanted her—wanted to win her over, keep her as the one woman he'd spend his life with. But now that the reality that he was already insanely in love with her was washing over him, Justice began to doubt himself—and his worthiness to own her.

He'd lied to her, after all—flat out lied to her about what his job was at the village. And he suspected that Baylee Cabot wasn't one to have any patience with liars. But what else could he do? It was his job, and it was the nature of his job to keep secrets—to protect people, not only physically but psychologically and emotionally. What would Baylee do if she knew how close the Jack the Ripper killer was to her? Would she sleep better at night? Would she worry less about the dangers of the world? Hell no! And that's what he did—protected people from harm as well as worry.

"Baylee?" he mumbled against her cheek once he'd broken the seal of their lips.

"Yes," she breathed against his neck.

"You know how I told you I work for a bureau?" he tentatively began.

"Yes," she breathed again, causing the flesh at his neck to warm and goose bumps to break out over his body.

"Well, I think you should know that it's kind of, like...*the* bureau," he ventured.

She looked up at him then, frowning a little. "What do you mean?" she asked. Her eyebrows arched, and she asked, "Do you mean, like, literally the FBI or something?"

Justice called on his courage and said, "Not 'or something.' The actual FBI."

He watched her eyes widen as understanding washed over her. "But...but why would the FBI have chimney sweep security guards posted at the Dickens Village?"

Again Justice mustered his courage. "If I say that I can't tell you yet...what will you do?"

Baylee studied his expression for a moment—entirely awed by what she saw there. Did he actually think the fact that he worked for the FBI would change the way she was reacting to him—the way she was feeling about him? But he did. She could see it in his eyes.

"If you say you can't tell me why you're at the Dickens Village every day dressed up like a sexy chimney sweep," she began. Slipping her arms under his to embrace him and pull him more tightly against her once more, she smiled and said, "I'd say, 'Okay. So let's get back to what we were doing.' That's what I'd do."

Baylee saw the relief wash over him as he smiled. "Okay then, my little bell-ringer," he mumbled.

"Pucker up and hold on tight. I'm about to ring your bell like it's never been rung."

Baylee giggled as Justice bent, kissing her neck a moment before his mouth returned to owning hers. Briefly the thought flittered through her mind that something big must be up concerning the Dickens Village, but it was fleeting. After all, what woman in her right mind would want to worry about something so inconsequential when she had Justice Kincaid in her arms?

CHAPTER EIGHT

"Three more victims since Thanksgiving," Brian said as he handed case files to the men. "This guy is really stepping it up. We've got to find him."

"Well, why are we wasting our time?" Tristan growled. "We should be out hunting this guy down, not dressed up like a bunch of idiots and hanging around at some stupid theme park!"

"If you'll refer to the new information on the last three victims, Holloway," Brain said, "you'll see that every one of them had visited the Dickens Village more than twice in the past two weeks. One woman even worked there for a day. She filled in at one of the vendor carts for a sick employee. The Dickens Village has definitely become this bastard's hunting ground." Slamming a file on the table in front of Tristan, Brian shouted, "So why the hell haven't we got him yet? We're the ones screwing up, Holloway! He's right under our noses, and we haven't seen him! So quit whining about the fact that we're here, step up to the plate, and catch the son of a—"

"Okay, okay," Tristan interrupted. "Sorry. I'm just sick of this guy. He's entirely eluding us. It doesn't make any sense."

"Maybe we're not profiling this correctly," Justice mumbled. He flipped through the file, again sickened by the fact that each and every Jack the Ripper copycat victim was a pretty brunette between the ages of eighteen and twenty-five. He was starting to have nightmares about the fact that Baylee fit the killer's victim profile so flawlessly. The FBI had to catch him—or he did.

"What do you mean?" Brian asked.

"I don't know. Something just doesn't fit," he mumbled. He thought for a moment. "I mean, sure, this guy started out in New York, then moved to Atlanta, then Dallas...but what if those were places outside his territory? What if he's a local boy? What if the Dickens Village is what set him off in the first place?" Justice flipped through the file he held. "Look—twenty-one victims...and the last thirteen have been killed or found within a five-mile radius of the Dickens Village. And as far as dates are concerned, all thirteen of the local murders occurred since November first...the day the Dickens Village launched its holiday season." Justice nodded, suddenly more positive than ever that his suspicions were correct. "We're looking for a local perp. The first eight murders...I think he was just waiting for the Dickens Village's holiday season to begin... practicing his methods before he started shooting fish in a barrel, so to speak."

Brian frowned for a moment. Then taking his cell

phone from the holster at his belt, he nodded and mumbled, "I'm gonna call D.C....have them rework the profile a bit. I think you're right, Kincaid. This guy is feeding out of a homemade trough."

Tristan looked to Justice, arching one inquisitive eyebrow. "So you've gone all psychological profiler on me now?"

Justice shook his head. "No. I just want this guy out of commission. He's whipping up on us, and women are dying because of it."

"Not just dying, man," Tristan sighed as he studied the police photos of the most recent victim. "They're being tortured, mutilated, and *then* dying."

"Thanks for pointing out the obvious, Tristan," Justice grumbled.

"Come on, man. What's with you?" Tristan asked. "Candice and I never see you and Baylee anymore. What? Do you guys just spend every free moment together?"

"Absolutely," Justice said. "And yet, *you* know how few free moments this team gets." He sighed with frustration. "I want this over. I want this guy dead so I can..."

"So you can what?" Tristan prodded when Justice paused.

"So I can move on to something else," Justice said, rising from his chair.

Tristan stood up as well. "Yeah. The chimney sweep gig is getting old." Tristan looked to Justice, his expression serious. "And though I put on the idiot clown, joking and laughing and complaining, it's because this guy gets under my skin...and he scares me where certain cute little carolers are concerned."

"Yeah," Justice agreed. "We need to put this bastard six feet under."

Tristan nodded, and Justice tried to calm the anxiety that had taken root in his gut. Christmas was only two weeks away, and he'd hoped to be able to give Baylee a gift she'd never see coming. But with all the time and energy the team was spending on surveillance, briefings, and research, Justice wasn't sure he should even travel down the road he wanted to travel with Baylee—at least, not yet. He was too tired, angry, and busy working all the time to have a moment to really consider his own future—and hers.

Justice approached Brian and in a whisper asked, "Are we done for now?"

Brian was still on the phone with Washington, but he nodded and made a gesture indicating the briefing was indeed over.

"Where're you off to, bra?" Tristan asked.

But Justice only grinned. "Where do you think?"

"Geez, man!" Tristan chuckled. "Don't you think about anything but Baylee these days?"

"Nope," Justice answered as he hurried out of the briefing room of the FBI field office. And it was true. Justice found that, of late, he only ever had one of two things on his mind—Baylee Cabot and catching the Jack the Ripper copycat, in that order.

Climbing into his truck, he roared out of the field

office parking lot and onto the main road. He'd made plans to meet Baylee during her fifteen-minute break at the Dickens Village before his next shift began. If he hurried, he'd make it—and since even one moment with Baylee was worth anything, he'd meet her or die trying!

❦

Baylee smiled as she watched the ethereally handsome chimney sweep saunter toward her. Most of the time she still couldn't believe Justice Kincaid was hers—her boyfriend anyway. But it was true! Since the night more than a month before—the night they'd watched the corny Christmas movie on TV at his house—she and Justice had been nearly inseparable during what little free time he had. It was crazy how many hours he was working, and Baylee hated it. Yet she knew that a lot of jobs and careers escalated in demands of time and stress when the holidays were approaching, and so she tried to be as patient as she could—to simply savor every moment she could spend with Justice, instead of resenting all the ones she couldn't.

Naturally, Baylee spent a lot of time wondering where her relationship with Justice would lead. The truth was that if he asked her that minute to marry him, she'd fling her arms around his neck and beg him to carry her off to the justice of the peace right that minute. But she wasn't sure his feelings were as deeply solidified as hers. Certainly he appeared to be as in love with her as any man could be in love with a woman, but the little nagging doubt that keeps everyone from being perfectly positive about something was always at the back of her mind.

And yet, as Justice advanced and reached her, gathering her into his arms and forcing her into the little alleyway nearby, Baylee sighed with renewed hope when she saw the affection and desire so profoundly visible in his beautiful green eyes.

"Hey, pretty baby," he mumbled against her mouth. His face was cold, chilled from having been walking in the cold air. But his lips and mouth were as warm as a radiator.

Over and over Justice kissed her—passionately, demandingly, thirstily—and Baylee wished he would never, never stop!

"I missed you," he mumbled against her mouth when he allowed a pause in their exchange for her to catch her breath.

"I missed you more," she breathed, tightening her embrace around his neck.

"Three weeks and you're done with this gig, right?" he said. "I can't wait until you're finished and only have your day ring-a-ding dinging to do."

"But what about you?" Baylee asked. "Won't you be finished here then too?"

"It depends," he said, brushing a hair from her face with the back of his hand.

"On what?" she asked. She knew the FBI was at the Dickens Village for a reason, but since she also knew that Justice couldn't tell her what the reason was, she hadn't pressed him. But now—knowing that the

Hampton Handbell Ringers and Carolers would be finished with their engagement at the Dickens Village, she'd hoped Justice's shifts would go back to normal as well.

"On some…stuff," Justice answered, and Baylee knew she couldn't press him about it. He grinned. "But…I'm only working one shift tomorrow," he informed her. "So that means, since you're off tomorrow too, we can hang out all night long. What do you say? Maybe there's a corny Christmas flick on we could watch, huh?"

"I say yes," Baylee giggled. "Don't I always say yes to you, Mr. Chimney Sweep?"

"Let's hope so," Justice chuckled. "Oh, I certainly hope so."

He kissed her again—long, deep, and hungrily. Then, releasing her and taking only her hand, he asked, "So how was your day, sugar plum?"

Baylee smiled. "Just fine," she answered. "Rather uneventful, in fact. How about you?"

Justice sighed. Oh, what he wouldn't give for the day to have been eventful—his team might have tagged and captured the Jack the Ripper killer. But unfortunately, everything had been as mundane as usual.

"Pretty uneventful as well, I'm afraid," he told her.

Baylee laughed and grasped his arm as they walked along the alleyway. "Well, how about you come over tomorrow before we watch our next wonderfully romantic made-for-TV Christmas show and help me decorate the rest of the gingerbread people cookies I made today?"

Justice laughed. "Yes!" he exclaimed with added dramatics. "That's exactly what I wanted to do on my only single-shift day." He looked at her and winked. "Provided there'll be cookie frosting available to lick off your lips."

"I'm sure I can arrange something," Baylee giggled.

Justice studied her a moment, wondering what he'd ever done in life to earn or deserve the love of a woman like Baylee. She was so beautiful—and not just her face and body. Everything about her was beautiful. From the way she rang her little handbells, to her voice, to the kindness she always, always displayed, to her witty sense of humor. All of her—that's what Justice loved— every inch and characteristic of Baylee Cabot.

"Oh, you guys are adorable!" an older woman exclaimed, rushing up to Baylee and Justice unexpectedly. "Would you mind if I took your picture?"

"Um…of course not," Justice stammered, uncertain as to whether he'd responded correctly. Looking to Baylee, he asked, "Do you mind, baby?"

"Of course I don't mind," Baylee giggled.

"Oh, thank you so much!" the woman gushed. "You guys are just too charming for words! The chimney sweep and the Christmas caroler—it's like a fairy tale!"

"Here, baby," Justice chuckled, brushing soot from Baylee's face. Leaning close to her, he whispered, "You better wipe that soot off your face. It looks like you've been necking with a chimney sweep or something."

Baylee giggled, allowing him to brush the soot from her face with his glove. Justice put his arm around her shoulders then, pulling her close to him so that the woman could take their photograph. Baylee was warm and smelled like apple cider and frosted snow, and Justice wished he could keep her there next to him, safe in his arms forever. He wished the Jack the Ripper killer would curl up and die somewhere so that at least one anxiety for Baylee's well-being would evaporate.

"Say cheese!" the enthusiastic lady said as she pressed the shutter button of her digital camera. "One more!" she begged, not waiting for permission. She studied them a moment after she'd taken their photo, sighed with contentment, and said, "Thank you so much, you guys. You really are too perfect together."

"Thank you, ma'am," Justice said. He nodded politely to the woman as she hurried off.

Looking down to Baylee, he smiled. "We do make a perfect couple, don't we?"

"Absolutely!" Baylee giggled.

Lowering his voice then, Justice suggested, "Maybe we oughta think about making it permanent, huh?"

"What?" Baylee asked. Had she heard him correctly? And if she had, had she understood his insinuation?'

Justice bent, pressing a quick kiss to her mouth. "You heard me," he said. "Now, you have a good evening, my little bell-ringer," he chuckled. "I'll be watching you from the rooftops…while I'm dancing around like ol' Dick Van Dyke up there."

But Baylee could only nod. She was still stunned by what he'd said. Make it permanent? Surely there could be only one thing he meant, right? He'd implied they should get married, hadn't he?

As Baylee walked back to the Dickens Village square, she was numb all over—numb with disbelief, numb with bliss, numb with utter, complete, and overwhelming euphoria! She was in love with Justice Kincaid—oh, so thoroughly, supremely, and eternally in love with him. And she was beginning to believe that he was nearly as in love with her.

"Maybe we oughta think about making it permanent?" she repeated in a breathy whisper as she took her place in the handbell choir.

"What did you say?" Candice asked. But Mr. Hampton cleared his voice, indicating that all eyes should be on him.

"Later," Baylee mumbled to Candice.

As the Hampton Handbell Ringers and Carolers began to perform "Carol of the Bells," Baylee Cabot silently hoped that maybe her dreams of owning Justice Kincaid's heart forever would come true in time for Christmas. After all, there was nothing in all the world she wanted more than Justice.

❦

"Mmmm," Justice moaned as he kissed the cookie frosting from Baylee's lips the next afternoon. "You know," he began, pulling her against him, "you taste just like frosted gingerbread cookies today."

Baylee giggled—tried to keep the spoon in her left

hand and the spatula in her right hand from getting frosting on Justice's clothes as he bound her to him, drinking in the warm passion her mouth willingly offered.

"I'm never going to get these cookies finished with you here. You do realize that," she teased him when their mouths separated for a moment.

"So you're saying you want me to leave you alone?" he flirted. "You'd rather ice cookies than neck with your boyfriend?"

Baylee's smile broadened. She tossed the spoon and spatula she'd been using to mix more frosting onto the nearby kitchen table, wrapped her arms tightly around Justice's neck, and breathed, "Absolutely not!" a moment before she applied a coaxing, playful kiss to his mouth.

Kissing, kissing, and more kissing! It's almost all they'd done all day. For some reason, Baylee was unable to find any explanation for why she and Justice seemed to be so driven to do nothing but kiss that day—but they were! It was as if something had escalated, but she didn't quite know what. All she knew was that she had to be in his arms, had to feel his lips pressed to hers almost constantly for the five hours they'd been attempting to ice gingerbread people cookies and watch a corny Christmas movie on TV.

They'd somehow managed to make it through the animated version of "How the Grinch Stole Christmas" without locking lips once. But that brief half an hour was the longest span of time they'd managed to not be somehow interlaced since Justice had arrived!

All at once something Justice had said flittered through Baylee's mind, and she giggled, even for the playful passion raging between them.

"What's so funny?" he asked, smiling at her.

She smiled up at him—ran her fingers over his head and through his short hair. "I just can't believe your grandma's verbiage has settled into our vernacular."

"You mean the term 'necking'?" he asked, grinning.

"Yeah," she affirmed. "It doesn't seem that long ago that we were joking about how archaic and weird it was...and yet—"

"Here we are," Justice interrupted. "Just standing in your kitchen, necking."

Baylee laughed. "Exactly!"

"Well, it just so happens...that I like your neck," Justice mumbled as he began placing soft, moist kisses along Baylee's throat.

"Well, it just so happens that I like that you like my neck," she whispered.

"Then it all works out...all the necking that goes on between the chimney sweep and the caroler, right?" he said, kissing her cheek.

"Absolutely," she sighed.

The sound of Candice's assigned ringtone startled Baylee from her bliss, however.

Justice released Baylee with a sigh of disappointment and said, "Cyndi Lauper and 'Girls Just Wanna Have

Fun'—I guess Candice and Tristan aren't necking if she's calling you right now."

"I'm sorry, Justice," Baylee said, picking up her cell phone from the table. "Tristan is working, and she's a little rattled. It seems like some guy from the Dickens Village has a thing for her or something, and today she—"

A wave of nausea washed over Justice as he watched Baylee answer her phone—heard her say, "Hey, girl. What's going on?"

Baylee held up one index finger indicating she'd only be a minute. But as the ominous sense of dread continued to seep into his soul, Justice glanced out the window. It was already dark outside. According to the coroner's times of death on the Jack the Ripper copycat victims, the psychopathic murderer killed just after sundown.

"At your window? Are you sure, Candice?" Baylee exclaimed. "Well, have you called Tristan?"

Snatching the phone from Baylee's hand, Justice demanded, "Give me your address, Candice...now!"

Baylee was astonished by Justice's behavior—not angry or offended, just astonished. She watched as he listened to Candice a moment, obviously receiving the information he'd demanded from her.

"Make sure every window is locked, Candice... every door. And do not go outside until someone gets there, do you hear me?" Justice nearly growled. "Stay put…and stay on the phone with Baylee." Handing her cell phone back to Baylee, he ordered, "Do not hang up on her…no matter what she says or what you hear."

"O-okay," Baylee stammered.

She watched then as Justice pulled his own cell from the holster at his belt. He pressed one button and then said, "This is federal agent SSA Justice Kincaid. I have a line on our Jack the Ripper. Send federal agents and local police to 6181 Prairie Sunset Lane. The perp's possible target is Candice Jones, resident of that address. She reports seeing a man dressed in period clothing, looking at her through her window. A second possible target is Baylee Cabot, address 2984 Mystic Falls. I am with that possible target now, but send backup here as well. Notify Unit Chief Brian Reagan."

"Candice?" Baylee managed to breathe into her cell. "Are you all right?"

"Stay here, Baylee," Justice ordered.

Baylee watched as he reached down, drawing a small handgun from a holster built into his boot. "I'm just going to check your windows…make sure they're secured."

Baylee nodded and tried to listen as Candice asked her what was going on. "What was all that? Did I hear Justice say he was sending police over here?" Candice sobbed on the phone.

"Um…yes," Baylee managed. "Apparently this guy you told me you saw last night following you…well, maybe the fact that he was following you isn't as benign as we thought, Candice."

"Baylee! What should I do?" Candice cried.

"J-just do what Justice told you to do. Make sure the windows and doors are locked…and wait for the police to arrive. I'm sure they're close," Baylee answered as tears began to stream down her face.

"Who is this guy, Baylee?" Candice sobbed. "I'm scared! Justice sounded so…so…did I hear him say he's a federal agent? Is he, like, with like some—"

"He's FBI, Candice," Baylee interrupted. "I'm pretty sure all the chimney sweeps are FBI."

Justice returned then and began dimming all the lights in the kitchen and front rooms of Baylee's rental house.

He gestured to her that she should give him her cell again, and she complied. "Candice?" he began. "I want you to remain as calm as you possibly can. Federal agents and police are on their way, though you might not hear any sirens. Now, is there anywhere in your house you can…*wait* for them? Maybe a crawl space or attic? Somewhere someone couldn't find you easily?"

Baylee brushed tears from her face and listened as Candice began to fall apart on the phone.

"Candice!" Justice growled. "Do not melt! Not now. Just get to a more secure location and wait. You'll hear the agents identify themselves when they enter your house. Only then do you come out. Do you understand?"

Baylee watched as Justice nodded. "That sounds fine, Candice. That sounds perfect, in fact. Now you go in there, and stay quiet. I'll stay on the phone with you until the FBI or police arrive. Okay? Don't talk or make a sound. Just stay quiet."

"Justice?" Baylee cried in a whisper.

Reaching out, Justice pulled her into his embrace, even for her cell phone in one hand and his gun in the other. "Shhh. It'll be fine. It'll only take a few minutes for them to get there…and here." He kissed the top of her head and then led her into the kitchen. "Come on. Sit down here," he said, indicating she should sit down behind the small island between the sink counter and the front room. "Just sit here and wait with me," he said as he slid down to sit beside her. "It's going to be fine." He spoke into the phone next, "You okay, Candice? Good…good. Just wait. It'll be fine. They're almost to you. I'm sure they are almost to you."

"It'll be fine, baby," Justice whispered to Baylee. "I won't let anything happen to you. I love you. You know that, right? And you know I'd never let anything happen to you, don't you?" Baylee looked up into the now blazing green of his eyes and nodded. "Okay then," he said as he pulled her closer to him. "Candice…try not to gasp so loudly," he said quietly into the cell phone. "That's right. Just breathe deep…a deep breath and a slow exhale. They'll be there in a minute…a million cops and FBI guys, okay? You'll be fine. Just breathe… nice and slow. That's it."

Baylee closed her eyes—clung desperately to Justice, vowing she'd never let him go again. She didn't know all of what was going on, but she had heard enough buzzwords and terms to figure out that Candice might

146

have been targeted by a serial killer that had been all over the news the past couple of months. It seemed impossible—not merely improbable, but entirely impossible!

But as all the pieces began to fit together in her mind—the ex-military security forces at the Dickens Village, Justice telling her weeks ago that he worked for the FBI but couldn't reveal details of his current assignment, and the fact that Justice had referred to the serial killer as Jack the Ripper when he'd called in about Candice—it all made sense in that moment.

"You're FB*I* FBI aren't you, Justice?" she whispered to him.

"Yeah," he answered, pulling her closer to him.

There was a noise then—like someone was messing with the doorknob of the front door.

"Hold this," Justice whispered, handing Baylee her cell once more.

Baylee stopped breathing as she watched Justice shift the safety on his gun—watched him take hold of it with two hands and look around the kitchen island toward the front door.

"SSA Kincaid?" a voice from the other side of the door called. "This is federal agent Javiar Morales informing you that the perimeter is secure."

Justice exhaled a relieved sigh and looked to Baylee.

"Everything is okay, baby. Breathe!" was the last thing she heard him say.

CHAPTER NINE

The Jack the Ripper copycat killer had chosen "death by cop." When police and federal agents arrived at Candice's house, they indeed did find a man, dressed in the period clothing common to the employees of the Dickens Village, lurking nearby. Yet when he was approached and told to surrender, he drew a pistol from somewhere within the folds of his black cape and began firing at police. Thus one of the most prolific serial killers of the new century was shot and killed.

Candice was found hiding in her kitchen pantry, in a state of shock. And even though she'd recovered by the time the ambulance arrived, she was taken to the hospital for observation and evaluation.

Baylee awoke from the short fainting spell that holding her breath had caused to find herself safely in Justice's arms and surrounded by police and FBI agents. The Hampton Handbell Ringers and Carolers missed their scheduled performance times at the Dickens Village that night, for it was closed to visitors while the

FBI interviewed every employee and vendor and went over the village with a fine-tooth comb.

Justice had stayed the night with Baylee and slept on the couch so that she'd feel safe and secure and be able to sleep. Yet by morning, Baylee was ready to leave the terrifying, though brief, experience behind her. Though it was terrifying to know Candice had been targeted by a serial killer—though Baylee knew she may have been a target as well—she also knew that no good would come from her hiding away and trembling in fear for the rest of her life. One thing was still true the day after the Jack the Ripper copycat was found—Baylee loved Justice more than anything, and all she wanted was to be with him.

Yet the next evening, as she performed with the Hampton Handbell Ringers (minus Candice, who still needed some time to emotionally heal), she thought the village felt lonesome and bare without the silhouettes of the chimney sweeps on the rooftops. Baylee knew no one else felt the emptiness she did—at least not the way she did. She wondered if all the employees might have felt a little more secure had the FBI had allowed the team of chimney sweep agents to stay on for a few days. But they hadn't, and Justice has returned to the FBI field office to work on the details and follow-ups of the Jack the Ripper copycat case.

The only good thing about Justice's not being at the Dickens Village every day was that on the evenings the Handbell Ringers weren't performing he and Baylee could spend their time together.

Baylee was relieved to discover that nothing had changed between them because of the drama or his not being at the Dickens Village with her. If anything, they seemed even more comfortable together, and she figured it was because Jack the Ripper wasn't always lurking in the back of his mind.

Thus, one week before Christmas found Justice at Baylee's house—both of them watching *A Christmas Story* as they wrapped gifts together.

"So you're just going to wrap up that Beretta and stick it under your grandma's tree? Just like that?" Baylee asked as she watched Justice awkwardly try to tie a decent wire ribbon bow around the gift he'd just wrapped.

"Well, sure," he said. "What else would I do?"

Baylee giggled. "I guess you're right. It's a Christmas gift, after all."

"Absolutely," Justice agreed.

He sighed as he finished tying a pathetic bow. "I do need to tell you something, baby," he began. By the sound in his voice, Baylee knew it wasn't good news he was about to reveal. Every shred of apprehension that was wafting around in her body seemed to fuse together into one giant ball of anxiety. What was he about to say? For a moment she worried that he was going to break up with her. It was the worst thing she could conceive, and she began to tremble a little.

"Yeah?" she prodded, though she wished she didn't have to hear whatever it was that was coming.

"I've got to report to DC," he said. "I'll be gone until New Year's Eve."

Baylee exhaled a breath of relief and mumbled, "Oh, good!"

"What?" Justice asked, looking at her with a hurt frown puckering his brow.

"I mean…I thought it was going to be something else…something really, really bad," she explained.

"Like what?" he asked. "I thought you'd be upset that I wouldn't be here for Christmas."

"I am!" she assured him, taking hold of his arm. "I just thought…I thought…"

"You thought what?" he urged, still looking at her as if he were a hurt puppy.

"I thought you were going to break up with me," she confessed.

"What?" he exclaimed. "You're kidding, right?"

Baylee shrugged. "I tried to think of the worst thing you could say to me…and that's what I thought of."

"Baylee," he breathed, taking her face between his hands. He smiled and chuckled a little. "But you know what's kind of funny about this?"

"What?" she asked, gazing into his dreamy peacock-green eyes.

"I was afraid you'd dump me last week when I had to shed the chimney sweep outfit for good," he told her.

"What?" it was her turn to ask.

Justice shrugged. "I was kind of afraid that whatever spell I'd managed to cast over you would disappear or something…that the chimney sweep charm would be gone and you'd dropkick me to the curb."

Baylee put her arms around his neck and stared into his preposterously handsome face. "Dropkick you to the curb?" she asked. "The chimney sweep charm gone? Your charm goes far, far beyond your cute little chimney sweep costume, Justice Kincaid."

"Really?" he asked as his lips pressed a warm kiss to hers.

"Absolutely!" she assured him as she kissed him in return.

"Well, just in case it did…I got you this for Christmas," he said. Reaching over to where his leather jacket lay on the sofa, he reached into his pocket and removed a tiny plastic bag. As he handed the small bag to her, he said, "I'll need to take your bracelet to the jeweler's before I leave. He said they have to solder it onto your bracelet or something."

Opening the small plastic back, Baylee giggled with delight when she dumped the contents into her hand and saw the beautiful silver chimney sweep charm tumble onto her palm.

Gasping with delight, she exclaimed, "A chimney sweep charm? Oh, Justice! I love it!" She threw her arms around his neck again, hugging him tightly and kissing his cheek. "It's perfect! It's so, so, *so* perfect!"

Justice chuckled and said, "I figure the jeweler can put it right next to that little Victorian caroler one you bought at the Dickens Village, and then your caroler and my chimney sweep can neck forever on your wrist."

Baylee laughed, hugged him again, brushed the tears of joy from the corners of her eyes, and sighed. "Justice...it's so perfect! Look at his little top hat and chimney sweep brush! Where did you find this?"

"The jeweler had to order it from somewhere in England," he answered. "I was afraid it wouldn't get here before I had to leave, and I wanted to give it to you before I did."

"And why is it that I can't just attach it?" Baylee mumbled to herself as she studied the charm. "Oh, I see. They need to still make a hole for the charm ring. Is that it?"

"Yeah, I guess," Justice said. "All I know is he told me to bring it in with whatever bracelet you want it attached to. Do you trust me enough to take it in? He says he can have it done by the time I get back if I take it in tomorrow morning before I leave."

"Tomorrow morning?" Baylee exclaimed, suddenly so disheartened she felt depressed.

Justice smiled and caressed her soft cheek with the back of his hand. A man could drown in the brown of Baylee Cabot's eyes—in the warmth of her embrace and the flavor of her mouth. Justice thought it would be a good way to go—drowning in the arms of the woman he loved.

Her pretty eyes filled with tears, and it made his heart ache, but he had to report to DC. It was unavoidable. "I'll be back as soon as I can. And that leads me to my next question. What are you doing New Year's Eve, you little bell-ringer, you?"

She smiled at him and answered, "Making out with my handsome FBI lover."

"You mean *necking* with your charming chimney sweep lover?" he corrected.

"Either or," she giggled.

He had to taste her then. Enough with wrapping gifts and talking about chimney sweep charms. Gathering Baylee into his arms, Justice ground his mouth to hers in a loving, wanting, impassioned kiss. Goose bumps rippled over his arms and legs as she kissed him with just as much love, wanting, and passion.

Suddenly, however, she pushed at his chest, broke the seal of their lips, and gasped.

"What's the matter?" he asked, concerned.

"All I got you is a new boot knife for your collection," she confessed.

Justice laughed and pulled her against him again. "I love you, Baylee Cabot," he mumbled against her mouth.

"I love you more," she breathed a moment before she took his breath away with her ambrosial kiss.

CHAPTER TEN

It was the longest twelve days of Baylee's life—the miserable twelve days that Justice was in Washington DC. The entire time he'd been gone, she'd done nothing but worry and fret, miss him, and long for New Year's Eve and his return. No amount of handbell ringing and caroling had served to distract her. None of the Christmas parties she'd attended felt fun, and no other gift she'd opened on Christmas morning with her parents seemed nearly as wonderful as the chimney sweep charm she knew was waiting with her bracelet at the jeweler's. She'd even lost four pounds in the time Justice had been gone for missing him so badly.

But now he was nearly back with her. He'd called when his plane had landed—nearly an hour before— and said he'd pick up her bracelet on his way to spend New Year's Eve with her at her place. Baylee had spent all day cooking—making snacks for her and Justice to enjoy—and roasting a ham to go with the potato dish she'd made for their dinner together.

She and Justice had been planning their New Year's

Eve since the day he left, having both agreed they'd rather stay in together all alone than attend the big to-do at the Dickens Village with everyone else. After all, they loved each other—liked each other's company more than anything else. Thus, they'd figured, why bother with socializing on such a crazy night as New Year's Eve tended to be?

Baylee heard his truck pull into her driveway, and a wave of emotion broke over her, causing tears of joy to spring to her eyes and goose bumps to race over every inch of her flesh. She heard the sound of his boots and opened the front door to be met by not only the sight of the most handsome man ever born but also an embrace and kiss that put any *The Princess Bride* kiss to shame!

Lifting Baylee off her feet as they kissed, Justice stepped into the house, kicking the door shut with his foot as he continued to nearly maul her with the mouth-to-mouth release of his pent-up desire.

"I missed you, I missed you, I missed you!" Baylee squealed as Justice kissed her cheeks, her forehead, her mouth, her neck, and the tip of her nose.

"I missed you more," he claimed, taking her mouth again. "Oh, you taste *so* good, Baylee Cabot!"

He was back! He was there in her arms, and Baylee felt her body breathe easier and relax a little for the first time in nearly two weeks. She couldn't seem to hug him tightly enough—couldn't seem to kiss him long enough. They paused in their affectionate exchange long enough for Justice to remove his coat, and then

Baylee giggled as he pushed her back against the wall and ravished her with hot, moist kisses of desire.

"Mmm," he moaned at last. "You smell so good."

Baylee giggled, "That's not me. That's the ham and potatoes."

"Nope...I'm pretty sure it's you," Justice teased. "It's making me hungry."

Again Baylee laughed. Playfully slapping him on one shoulder, she disengaged herself from his arms and started toward the kitchen.

"That's because of the ham and potatoes," she giggled as she began to take the ham out of the oven. "I figured you'd be way hungry, so I made a ton of dinner for us...and some snacks and stuff for later."

"Did you get the movie?" he asked, following her into the kitchen.

"Of course," she said as he took hold of her elbow, turned her to face him, pushed her back against the counter, and kissed her again.

"And you didn't change your mind about me while I was gone?" he asked, his expression going serious for a moment.

"Why? Did you change your mind about me while you were gone?" Baylee asked, suddenly anxious.

"Am I acting like I changed my mind about you, sugar plum?" he asked, kissing her.

Baylee smiled. He loved her. She could see it in the smoldering green of his beautiful eyes.

"Am I acting like *I* changed my mind about *you?*" she countered.

Justice smiled. "So the chimney sweep charm didn't wear off then?"

"Never," she breathed. Suddenly remembering the bracelet charm Justice had given her for Christmas, she asked, "Did you have a chance to stop and pick up my bracelet?"

"Absolutely," Justice said. He released her and went to where he'd discarded his leather jacket. He picked it up, rummaging around in one pocket.

"Here you go," he said as he returned to her. Holding the clasp of the bracelet clutched in his fist, he held it above her head and teased, "What'll you give me for it?"

Baylee smiled, delighted by his teasing. "What do you want for it?" she flirted.

"Only your heart," he said. "And everything else that comes with it," he added as Baylee saw that more than the chimney sweep charm had been added to her bracelet.

Tears sprung to her eyes, and she couldn't breathe as she stared at the chocolate diamond solitaire ring that had been threaded onto the bracelet's chain.

"It's a...it's a ring," she whispered.

"It's an engagement ring, to be exact...and you better breathe, baby," he chuckled. "Remember what happened last time you held your breath too long."

"Justice," was all Baylee could say. Only his name. It was all that would come out of her mouth as she stood in stunned, yet euphoric, astonishment.

"Here," he said, unlatching the bracelet's clasp and

removing the ring from its chain. "Maybe I better try it this way."

Dropping to one knee, Justice took Baylee's left hand in his, slipped her charm bracelet onto her wrist and the chocolate diamond onto her left ring finger, and asked, "Baylee Cabot, you little bell-ringer, you... will you marry me?"

As tears streamed down her cheeks, Baylee whispered, "Absolutely!" with just the perfect amount of blissful enthusiasm.

"Then feed me your ham and potatoes, wife-to be," Justice said, standing and gathering a sobbing Baylee into his arms. "Before my barely bridled desire consumes *you* first." Justice kissed her then—once again ravishing her mouth with passionate exchanges of love and desperate wanting.

As they continued to kiss, Baylee was somewhat aware of the charm bracelet at her wrist, very aware of the chocolate diamond on her finger, and thoroughly aware of how lucky she was to own the love of the handsome federal agent who had cast his chimney sweep charm and captured her heart.

AUTHOR'S NOTE

Yes, I love handbells and "Carol of the Bells" performed on them. Yes, I love Dick Van Dyke as the chimney sweep Bert in *Mary Poppins*—and I was totally disappointed when Mary Poppins drifted off at the end of the movie instead of staying to enjoy a mad, passionate love affair with Bert. Yes, I love hot chocolate—and with a soft peppermint stick to stir it with. Yes, I love and adore our military veterans and think they deserve more respect and adulation. Yes, I love Christmas and everything about it. And yes, I hope I've written something just easy and fun—romantic and kissy—something that enabled you to find a moment of respite this holiday season. Yes, I always wanted a charm bracelet of my own. (Thank you, Lisa J., for making that dream come true!) And yes, I could babble on and on about what inspired me while writing this little novella, *The Chimney Sweep Charm*.

But since I did intend for this book to be a little lighthearted holiday escape, I thought I'd skew off onto something a little different in this Author's Note: that being the incredible venue of amusement the cover artist and I enjoyed during our collaboration on the cover for *The Chimney Sweep Charm*—i.e., the Golden Man image.

As Sheri (the brilliant and singular graphics designer for my book covers) and I were searching through hundreds, then thousands, of images to be submitted as possibilities for the cover of *The Chimney Sweep Charm*, we began to experience a frustration we hadn't ever encountered before. We tried searching everywhere for just the right images! Every chimney sweep graphic anybody could find, we considered it. Every Old London-looking rooftop scene, every brick chimney photo—basically anything that could have had something to do with the book—we considered it.

"How about a brass handbell?" one of us suggested. "How about just this sooty-looking chimney sweep's hand?" The possibilities were endless, but the available graphics were few, and I couldn't like anything that was being presented.

With immense discouragement washing over me, I finally *settled* on a couple of images and asked Sheri, "Can you do something with *these*?" She agreed to try. However, her guts were churning with dissatisfaction as well. Nothing made Sheri feel positive, and nothing said "Justice Kincaid, the FBI chimney sweep," to me.

And so, one night as I was swathed in thinking I really would just have to settle when it came to a cover for *The Chimney Sweep Charm*, I sat down at my computer and began searching through more photographs—looking for anything that might spark my imagination or Sheri's.

Well, I must've blown a kiss to a chimney sweep myself sometime last summer because that night the first image that came up on my computer was of a guy who looked as if he might have potential for something someday where book covers were concerned. I wasn't all that excited about it, but I began to think (knowing Sheri's mad graphic design skill and creative majesty) that maybe she could fuse two images somehow the way she'd done with the new *Divine Deception* cover. Maybe the cover didn't need to be *just* a chimney sweep or *just* a rooftop scene. Maybe it could be made up of both.

Now, naturally, I knew we were never going to find an image of a handsome chimney sweep, stationed on an old Camden Town rooftop, peering through a pair of FBI-issued binoculars, but maybe (between Sheri and me and our common creative juices) we could create something similar.

So I e-mailed the guy's image to Sheri and began clicking around on other images while I waited for her response. I decided to see what other images this particular photographer might have to offer. I clicked on another image, and voilà! Holy better image, Batman! It was the same model the photographer had used in the first image, but this time he was kind of banged up, shirtless, and holding a sword, and the photo was entitled "Warrior."

Hmmm, I thought. *Maybe Sheri could use this one somehow...only not the shirtless part.* So I e-mailed the image to Sheri and continued to click around on the same photographer's images as I waited for her to respond to the second image I found.

However, the next image I clicked nearly reached out and slapped me in the face. Not only was it a great angle but the guy's face was smudged up just like a chimney sweep's!

"This is it!" I said aloud and instantly sent Sheri an e-mail with a subject line of something like *Hold the phone! Here it is!*

Sheri called me the second she opened the e-mail with Justice Kincaid's picture and agreed. We had found one of the images for the cover of *The Chimney Sweep Charm*!

So what's the big deal? you may be thinking. Well, I'll tell you: in truth, there were several big deals. First, I had to decide if I were really going to allow a significant portion of a person's face to dominate a cover. (You know how I like to leave things to the imagination, right?) Second, there were a couple of challenges with the image regarding Sheri's designing process. The photograph, in its entirety, is not only a shirtless one but the lighting was all orange and warm. Plus, the guy's skin was sort of glittery, and his elbow looked like it was jammed up against a glass wall or something.

However, Sheri and I both agreed—the Golden Man (as we affectionately nicknamed him) was perfect for the cover of *The Chimney Sweep Charm*. Glittery skin, neked shoulder, and orange lighting or not, the Golden Man won us over!

The challenge then fell to Sheri to perform miracles with the Golden Man while I tried to approve of a Christmassy rooftops image.

Covers are important to me—paramount! I've been so very disappointed in the past when things were beyond my decision or control that now that I'm able to accept or veto the covers for my books once again, I'm nearly obsessed with needing them to convey not only what the book is about but what I'm feeling as well. Furthermore, I cannot tell you what it meant to me to finally be able to have an artist like Sheri Brady creating my covers. And as you can see, her cover of *The Chimney Sweep Charm* was a dream come true (at least for me).

I wish I'd kept all the e-mail exchanges during the cover process for this book—the hysterical comments about the Golden Man and "getting his lips just right" in the blended image. Sheri knew that if I were going to take an uncomfortable leap and put a face on one of my covers, I needed the constant reassurance that the guy in the image was worthy of being there. Consequently, her hysterical remarks in e-mails and on the phone kept me in stitches through the entire process of not only her creating the cover but also my getting over the anxiety of having a real face on it!

Sheri's witty comments—such as "I spent hours with the Golden Man. His lips drew me in," or "I tried rubbing the glitter off his shoulder and running my fingers through his hair to straighten it"—made me giggle and enjoy moments of the same sort of worry-free escapism I hope the book offers to you. And *that's* why I even bothered telling you this little "behind-the-scenes" story—because I hope that reading *The Chimney Sweep Charm* is for you exactly what the cover collaboration between me and Sheri was for me—an easy, lighthearted, fun, "everything is okay," "Christmastime is wonderful" escape. I know that the Golden Man and all of Sheri's hilarious remarks and work on the cover don't really mean anything to you out of context, but it's the way I felt when she and I were collaborating on it that I want to convey. So I hope that in some way, this little novella—though it's no profound work of fiction that will sit on the shelf next to *Jane Eyre* in years to come—gave you a little lift and let you escape the craziness of life, the worries, the stress. It's what I always hope when I write a book— that you'll smile and feel rested for a time because of it.

And finally—just so you can have a better idea of what Sheri started with and why she stayed up all night with the Golden Man working on his lips—here he is in glorious, old 1940s movie-star black-and-white.

Merry Christmas!
~Marcia Lynn McClure

My everlasting admiration, gratitude, and love…
To my husband, Kevin…
My inspiration…
My heart's desire…
The man of my every dream!

ABOUT THE AUTHOR

Marcia Lynn McClure's intoxicating succession of novels, novellas, and e-books—including *The Visions of Ransom Lake*, *A Crimson Frost*, *The Rogue Knight*, and most recently *The Pirate Ruse*—has established her as one of the most favored and engaging authors of true romance. Her unprecedented forte in weaving captivating stories of western, medieval, regency, and contemporary amour void of brusque intimacy has earned her the title "The Queen of Kissing."

Marcia, who was born in Albuquerque, New Mexico, has spent her life intrigued with people, history, love, and romance. A wife, mother, grandmother, family historian, poet, and author, Marcia Lynn McClure spins her tales of splendor for the sake of offering respite through the beauty, mirth, and delight of a worthwhile and wonderful story.

BIBLIOGRAPHY

A Better Reason to Fall in Love

A Crimson Frost

An Old-Fashioned Romance

Beneath the Honeysuckle Vine

Born for Thorton's Sake

Daydreams

Desert Fire

Divine Deception

Dusty Britches

Kiss in the Dark

Kissing Cousins

Love Me

Saphyre Snow

Shackles of Honor

Sudden Storms

Sweet Cherry Ray

Take a Walk With Me

The Anthology of Premiere Novellas Romantic Vignettes

The Fragrance of her Name

The Haunting of Autumn Lake

The Heavenly Surrender

The Heavenly Surrender 10th Anniversary Special Edition

The Highwayman of Tanglewood

The Light of the Lovers' Moon

The Pirate Ruse

The Prairie Prince

The Rogue Knight

The Tide of the Mermaid Tears

A Better Reason to Fall in Love
Contemporary Romance

"Boom chicka wow wow!" Emmy whispered.

"Absolutely!" Tabby breathed as she watched Jagger Brodie saunter past.

She envied Jocelyn for a moment, knowing he was most likely on his way to drop something off on Jocelyn's desk—or to speak with her. Jocelyn got to talk with Jagger almost every day, whereas Tabby was lucky if he dropped graphics changes off to her once a week.

"Ba boom chicka wow wow!" Emmy whispered again. "He's sporting a red tie today! Ooo! The power tie! He must be feeling confident."

Tabby smiled, amused and yet simultaneously amazed at Emmy's observation. She'd noticed the red tie too. "There's a big marketing meeting this afternoon," she told Emmy. "I heard he's presenting some hard-nose material."

"Then that explains it," Emmy said, smiling. "Mr. Brodie's about to rock the company's world!"

"He already rocks mine...every time he walks by," Tabby whispered.

A Crimson Frost
Historical Romance

Beloved of her father, King Dacian, and adored by her people, the Scarlet Princess Monet endeavored to serve her kingdom well—for the people of the Kingdom of Karvana were good and worthy of service. Long Monet had known that even her marriage would serve her people. Her husband would be chosen for her—for this was the way of royal existence.

Still, as any woman does—peasant or princess—Monet dreamt of owning true love—of owning choice in love. Thus, each time the raven-haired, sapphire-eyed, Crimson Knight of Karvana rode near, Monet knew regret—for in secret, she loved him—and she could not choose him.

As an arrogant king from another kingdom began to wage war against Karvana, Karvana's king, knights, and soldiers answered the challenge. The Princess Monet would also know battle. As the Crimson Knight battled with armor and blade, so the Scarlet Princess would battle in sacrifice and with secrets held. Thus, when the charge was given to preserve the heart of Karvana, Monet endeavored to serve her kingdom and forget her secreted love. Yet love is not so easily forgotten…

An Old-Fashioned Romance
Contemporary Romance

Life went along simply, if not rather monotonously, for Breck McCall. Her job was satisfying; she had true friends. But she felt empty—as if party of her soul was detached and lost to her. She longed for something—something that seemed to be missing.

Yet there were moments when Breck felt she might almost touch something wonderful. And most of those moments came while in the presence of her handsome, yet seemingly haunted boss—Reese Thatcher.

Beneath the Honeysuckle Vine
Historical Romance

Civil War—no one could flee from the nightmare of battle and the countless lives it devoured. Everyone had sacrificed—suffered profound misery and unimaginable loss. Vivianna Bartholomew was no exception. The war had torn her from her home— orphaned her. The merciless war seemed to take everything—even the man she loved. Still, Vivianna yet knew gratitude, for a kind friend had taken her in upon the death of her parents. Thus, she was cared for—even loved.

Yet as General Lee surrendered, signaling the war's imminent end—as Vivianna remained with the remnants of the Turner family—her soul clung to the letters written by her lost soldier—to his memory written in her heart. Could a woman ever heal from the loss of such a love? Could a woman's heart forget that it may find another? Vivianna Bartholomew thought not.

Still, it is often in the world that miracles occur— that love endures even after hope has been abandoned. Thus, one balmy Alabama morning—as two ragged soldiers wound the road toward the Turner house— Vivianna began to know—to know that miracles do exist—that love is never truly lost.

Born for Thorton's Sake
Historical Romance

Maria Castillo Holt…the only daughter of a valiant lord and his Spanish beauty. Following the tragic deaths of her parents, Maria would find herself spirited away by conniving kindred in an endurance of neglect and misery.

However, rescued at the age of thirteen by Brockton Thorton, the son of her father's devoted friend Lord Richard Thorton, Maria would at last find blessed reprieve. Further Brockton Thorton became, from that day forth, ever the absolute center of Maria's very existence. And as the blessed day of her sixteenth birthday dawned, Maria's dreams of owning her heart's desire seemed to become a blissful reality.

Yet a fiendish plotting intruded, and Maria's hopes of realized dreams were locked away within dark, impenetrable walls. Would Maria's dreams of life with the handsome and coveted Brockton Thorton die at the hands of a demon strength?

Daydreams
Contemporary Romance

Sayler Christy knew chances were slim to none that any of her silly little daydreams would ever actually come true—especially any daydreams involving Mr. Booker, the new patient—the handsome, older patient convalescing in her grandfather's rehabilitation center.

Yet, working as a candy striper at Rawlings Rehab, Sayler couldn't help but dream of belonging to Mr.

Booker—and Mr. Booker stole her heart—perhaps unintentionally—but with very little effort. Gorgeous, older, and entirely unobtainable, Sayler knew Mr. Booker would unknowingly enslave her heart for many years to come—for daydreams were nothing more than a cruel joke inflicted by life. All dreams—daydreams or otherwise—never came true. Did they?

Desert Fire
Historical Romance

She opened her eyes and beheld, for the first time, the face of Jackson McCall. Ruggedly handsome and her noble rescuer, he would, she knew in that moment, forever hold captive her heart as he then held her life in his protective arms.

Yet she was a nameless beauty, haunted by wisps of visions of the past. How could she ever hope he would return the passionate, devotional love she secreted for him when her very existence was a riddle?

Would Jackson McCall (handsome, fascinating, brooding) ever see her as anything more than a foundling—a burden to himself and his family? And with no memory of her own identity, how then could she release him from his apparent affliction of being her protector?

Divine Deception
Historical Romance

Life experience had harshly turned its cruel countenance on the young Fallon Ashby. Her father deceased and her mother suffering with a fatal disease, Fallon was given over to her uncle, Charles Ashby, until she would reach the age of independence.

Abused, neglected, and disheartened, Fallon found herself suddenly blessed with unexpected liberation at the hand of the mysterious Trader Donavon. A wealthy landowner and respected denizen of the town, Trader Donavon concealed his feature of face within the shadows of a black cowl.

When Fallon's secretive deliverer offered two choices of true escape from her uncle, her captive heart chose its own path. Thus, Fallon married the enormous structure of mortal man—without having seen the horrid secret he hid beneath an ominous hood.

But the malicious Charles Ashby, intent on avenging his own losses at Trader Donavon's hand, set out to destroy the husband that Fallon herself held secrets concerning. Would her wicked uncle succeed and perhaps annihilate the man that his niece secretly loved above all else?

Dusty Britches
Historical Romance

Angelina Hunter was serious-minded, and it was a good thing. Her father's ranch needed a woman who could endure the strenuous work of ranch life. Since her mother's death, Angelina had been that woman. She had no time for frivolity—no time for a less severe side of life. Not when there was so much to be done—

hired hands to feed, a widower father to care for, and an often ridiculously lighthearted younger sister to worry about. No. Angelina Hunter had no time for the things most young women her age enjoyed.

And yet, Angelina had not always been so hardened. There had been a time when she boasted a fun, flirtatious nature even more delightful than her sister Becca's—a time when her imagination soared with adventurous, romantic dreams. But that all ended years before at the hand of one man. Her heart turned to stone…safely becoming void of any emotion save impatience and indifference.

Until the day her dreams returned, the day the very maker of her broken heart rode back into her life. As the dust settled from the cattle drive that brought him back, would Angelina's heart be softened? Would she learn to hope again? Would her long-lost dreams become a blessed reality?

Kiss in the Dark

Contemporary Romance

"Boston," he mumbled.

"I mean…Logan…he's like the man of my dreams! Why would I blow it? What if…" Boston continued to babble.

"Boston," he said. The commanding sound of his voice caused Boston to cease in her prattling and look to him.

"What?" she asked, somewhat grateful he'd interrupted her panic attack.

He frowned and shook his head.

"Shut up," he said. "You're all worked up about nothing." He reached out, slipping one hand beneath her hair to the back of her neck.

Boston was so startled by his touch, she couldn't speak—she could only stare up into his mesmerizing green eyes. His hand was strong and warm, powerful and reassuring.

"If it freaks you out so much…just kiss in the dark," he said.

Boston watched as Vance put the heel of his free hand to the light switch. In an instant the room went black.

Kissing Cousins
Contemporary Romance

Poppy Amore loved her job waitressing at Good Ol' Days Family Restaurant. No one could ask for a better working environment. After all, her best friend Whitney worked there, and her boss, restaurant owner Mr. Dexter, was a kind, understanding, grandfatherly sort of man. Furthermore, the job allowed Poppy to linger in the company of Mr. Dexter's grandson Swaggart Moretti—the handsome and charismatic head cook at Good Ol' Days.

Secretly, Swaggart was far more to Poppy than just a man who was easy to look at. In truth, she had harbored a secret crush on him for years—since her freshman year in high school, in fact. And although the memory of her feelings—even the lingering truth of them—haunted Poppy the way a veiled, unrequited love always haunts a heart, she had learned to simply find joy in possessing a hidden, anonymous delight in merely being associated with Swaggart. Still, Poppy had begun to wonder if her heart would ever let go of Swaggart Moretti—if any other man in the world could ever turn her head.

When the dazzling, uber-fashionable Mark Lawson appeared one night at Good Ol' Days, however, Poppy began to believe that perhaps her attention and her heart would be distracted from Swaggart at last. Mark Lawson was every girl's fantasy—tall, uniquely handsome, financially well-off, and as charming as any prince ever to appear in fairy tales. He was kind, considerate, and, Poppy would find, a true, old-fashioned champion. Thus, Poppy Amore willingly allowed her heart and mind to follow Mark Lawson—to attempt to abandon the past and an unrequited love and begin to move on.

But all the world knows that real love is not so easily put off, and Poppy began to wonder if even a man so wonderful as Mark Lawson could truly drive Swaggart Moretti from her heart. Would Poppy Amore miss her one chance at happiness, all for the sake of an unfulfilled adolescent's dream?

Love Me
Contemporary Romance

Jacey Whittaker couldn't remember a time when she hadn't loved Scott Pendleton—the boy next door.

She couldn't remember a time when Scott hadn't been in her life—in her heart. Yet Scott was every other girl's dream too. How could Jacey possibly hope to win such a prize—the attention, the affections, the very heart of such a sought-after young man? Yet win him she did! He became the bliss of her youthful heart—at least for a time.

Still, some dreams live fulfilled—and some are lost. Loss changes the very soul of a being. Jacey wondered if her soul would ever rebound. Certainly, she went on—lived a happy life—if not so full and perfectly happy a life as she once lived. Yet she feared she would never recover—never get over Scott Pendleton—her first love.

Until the day a man walked into her apartment—into her apartment and into her heart. Would this man be the one to heal her broken heart? Would this man be her one true love?

Saphyre Snow
Historical Romance

Descended of a legendary line of strength and beauty, Saphyre Snow had once known happiness as princess of the Kingdom of Graces. Once a valiant king had ruled in wisdom—once a loving mother had spoken soft words of truth to her daughter. Yet a strange madness had poisoned great minds—a strange fever inviting Lord Death to linger. Soon it was even Lord Death sought to claim Saphyre Snow for his own—and all Saphyre loved seemed lost.

Thus, Saphyre fled—forced to leave all familiars for necessity of preserving her life. Alone, and without provision, Saphyre knew Lord Death might yet claim her—for how could a princess hope to best the Reaper himself?

Still, fate often provides rescue by extraordinary venues, and Saphyre was not delivered into the hands of Death—but into the hands of those hiding dark secrets in the depths of bruised and bloodied souls. Saphyre knew a measure of hope and asylum in the company of these battered vagabonds. Even she knew love—a secreted love—a forbidden love. Yet it was love itself—even held secret—that would again summon Lord Death to hunt the princess, Saphyre Snow.

Shackles of Honor
Historical Romance

Cassidy Shea's life was nothing if not serene. Loving parents and a doting brother provided happiness and innocent hope in dreaming as life's experience. Yes, life was blissful at her beloved home of Terrill.

Still, for all its beauty and tranquility…ever there was something intangible and evasive lurking in the shadows. And though Cassidy wasted little worry on it…still she sensed its existence, looming as a menacing fate bent on ruin.

And when one day a dark stranger appeared, Cassidy could no longer ignore the ominous whispers of the secrets surrounding her. Mason Carlisle, an angry, unpredictable man materialized…and seemingly with Cassidy's black fate at his heels.

Instantly Cassidy found herself thrust into a world completely unknown to her, wandering in a labyrinth of mystery and concealments. Serenity was vanquished… and with it, her dreams.

Or were all the secrets so guardedly kept from Cassidy…were they indeed the cloth, the very flax from which her dreams were spun? From which eternal bliss would be woven?

Sudden Storms
Historical Romance

Rivers Brighton was a wanderer—having nothing and belonging to no one. Still, by chance, Rivers found herself harboring for a time beneath the roof of the kind-hearted Jolee Gray and her remarkably attractive yet ever-grumbling brother, Paxton. Jolee had taken Rivers in, and Rivers had stayed.

Helplessly drawn to Paxton's alluring presence and unable to escape his astonishing hold over her, however, Rivers knew she was in danger of enduring great heartbreak and pain. Paxton appeared to find Rivers no more interesting than a brief cloudburst. Yet the man's spirit seemed to tether some great and devastating storm—a powerful tempest bridled within, waiting for the moment when it could rage full and free, perhaps destroying everything and everyone in its wake—particularly Rivers.

Could Rivers capture Paxton's attention long

enough to make his heart her own? Or would the storm brewing within him destroy her hopes and dreams of belonging to the only man she had ever loved?

Sweet Cherry Ray
Historical Romance

Cherry glanced at her pa, who frowned and slightly shook his head. Still, she couldn't help herself, and she leaned over and looked down the road.

She could see the rider and his horse—a large buckskin stallion. As he rode nearer, she studied his white shirt, black flat-brimmed hat, and double-breasted vest. Ever nearer he rode, and she fancied his pants were almost the same color as his horse, with silver buttons running down the outer leg. Cherry had seen a similar manner of dress before—on the Mexican vaqueros that often worked for her pa in the fall.

"Cherry," her pa scolded in a whisper as the stranger neared them.

She straightened and blushed, embarrassed by being as impolite in her staring as the other town folk were in theirs. It seemed everyone had stopped whatever they had been doing to walk out to the street and watch the stranger ride in.

No one spoke—the only sound was that of the breeze, a falcon's cry overhead and the rhythm of the rider's horse as it slowed to a trot.

Take a Walk with Me
Contemporary Romance

"Grandma?" Cozy called as she closed the front door behind her. She inhaled a deep breath—bathing in the warm, inviting scent of banana nut bread baking in the oven. "Grandma? Are you in here?"

"Cozy!" her grandma called in a loud whisper. "I'm in the kitchen. Hurry!"

Cozy frowned—her heart leapt as worry consumed her for a moment. Yet, as she hurried to the kitchen to find her grandma kneeling at the window that faced the new neighbors yard, and peering out with a pair of binoculars, she exhaled a sigh of relief.

"Grandma! You're still spying on him?" she giggled.

"Get down! They'll see us! Get down!" Dottie ordered in a whisper, waving one hand in a gesture that Cozy should duck.

Giggling with amusement at her grandma's latest antics, Cozy dropped to her hands and knees and crawled toward the window.

"Who'll see us?" she asked.

"Here," Dottie whispered, pausing only long enough to reach for a second set of binoculars sitting on the nearby counter. "These are for you." She smiled at Cozy—winked as a grin of mischief spread over her face. "And now…may I present the entertainment for this evening…Mr. Buckly hunk of burning love Bryant…and company."

Romantic Vignettes—The Anthology of Premiere Novellas
Historical Romance
Includes Three Novellas:

The Unobtainable One

Annette Jordan had accepted the unavoidable reality that she must toil as a governess to provide for herself. Thankfully, her charge was a joy—a vision of youthful beauty, owning a spirit of delight.

But it was Annette's employer, Lord Gareth Barrett, who proved to be the trial—for she soon found herself living in the all-too-cliché governess's dream of having fallen desperately in love with the man who provided her wages.

The child loved her—but could she endure watching hopelessly as the beautiful woman from a neighboring property won Lord Barrett's affections?

The General's Ambition

Seemingly overnight, Renee Millings found herself orphaned and married to the indescribably handsome, but ever frowning, Roque Montan. His father, The General, was obsessively determined that his lineage would continue posthaste—with or without consent of his son's new bride.

But when Roque reveals the existence of a sworn oath that will obstruct his father's ambition, will the villainous General conspire to ensure the future of his coveted progeny to be born by Renee himself? Will Renee find the only means of escape from the odious General to be that of his late wife—death? Or will the son find no tolerance for his father's diabolic plotting concerning the woman Roque legally terms his wife?

Indebted Deliverance

Chalyce LaSalle had been grateful to the handsome recluse, Race Trevelian, when he had delivered her from certain tragedy one frigid winter day. He was addictively attractive, powerful, and intriguing—and there was something else about him—an air of secreted internal torture. Yet, as the brutal character of her emancipator began to manifest, Chalyce commenced in wondering whether the fate she now faced would be any less insufferable than the one from which he had delivered her.

Still, his very essence beckoned hers. She was drawn to him and her soul whispered that his mind needed deliverance as desperately as she had needed rescue that cold winter's noon.

The Fragrance of Her Name

Historical Romance

Love—the miraculous, eternal bond that binds two souls together. Lauryn Kennsington knew the depth of it. Since the day of her eighth birthday, she had lived the power of true love—witnessed it with her own heart. She had talked with it—learned not even time or death can vanquish it. The Captain taught her these truths—and she loved him all the more for it.

Yet now—as a grown woman—Lauryn's dear

Captain's torment became her own. After ten years, Lauryn had not been able to help him find peace—the peace his lonely spirit so desperately needed—the peace he'd sought every moment since his death over fifty years before.

Still, what of her own peace? The time had come. Lauryn's heart longed to do the unthinkable—selfishly abandon her Captain for another—a mortal man who had stolen her heart—become her only desire.

Would Lauryn be able to put tormented spirits to rest and still be true to her own soul? Or, would she have to make a choice—a choice forcing her to sacrifice one true love for another?

The Haunting of Autumn Lake
Historical Romance

Autumn gasped as she looked up to see the third cowboy, slumping in his saddle. Blood was streaming from a wound in his left leg and had begun to dry on his chaps. His shirt was soaked with blood at the left shoulder, and more dried blood was matting the hair on his forehead, eyebrows, and cheek.

"My apologies, mister," the cowboy mumbled.

"Nothin' to apologize for, son," Ransom said. "But you better get on down here so Doc Sullivan can look you over."

"Yes, sir," the cowboy said.

Then, as he attempted to dismount, the full depth of his weakness from injury and no doubt blood loss was evident as he fell to the ground and groaned.

Autumn, owning a character twin to her mother, was not only prone to mischief and clumsiness but also thoroughly steeped with sympathetic compassion and empathy. Thus, instantly and without thinking, she dropped to her knees and moved the poor cowboy's head to rest in her lap.

"He needs to breathe, for one thing," she mumbled as her father hunkered down beside her.

Tenderly she tugged at the brown bandana covering the man's nose and mouth, gasping when he opened his eyes and looked at her.

Autumn Lake's heart skipped a beat—it skipped several beats—as she gazed into the deep blue of the man's eyes...

As the cowboy gazed at Autumn a moment more, he smiled and said, "Heaven's got better-lookin' angels than I expected." But it wasn't his fevered mind's words that astonished her. It wasn't even the fact that the man obviously thought he was at death's door, or beyond it. It was the sight of his smile—his broad smile, his unusually white teeth—and more than anything, it was the clefts he bore on each cheek—the bewilderingly attractive dimples the man owned—that left Autumn breathless and staring at him. This wounded cowboy was flabbergastingly handsome! He was violently attractive, and Autumn had to inwardly whisper to herself to draw a breath...

The Heavenly Surrender
Historical Romance

Genieva Bankmans had willfully agreed to the arrangement. She had given her word, and she would not dishonor it. But when she saw, for the first time, the man whose advertisement she had answered... she was desperately intimidated. The handsome and commanding Brevan McLean was not what she had expected. He was not the sort of man she had reconciled herself to marrying.

This man, this stranger whose name Genieva now bore, was strong-willed, quick-tempered, and expectant of much from his new wife. Brevan McLean did not deny he had married her for very practical reasons only. He merely wanted any woman whose hard work would provide him assistance with the brutal demands of farm life.

But Genieva would learn there were far darker things, grave secrets held unspoken by Brevan McLean concerning his family and his land. Genieva Bankmans McLean was to find herself in the midst of treachery, violence, and villainy with her estranged husband deeply entangled in it.

The Highwayman of Tanglewood
Historical Romance

A chambermaid in the house of Tremeshton, Faris Shayhan well knew torment, despair, and trepidation. To Faris it seemed the future stretched long and desolate before her—bleak and as dark as a lonesome midnight path. Still, the moon oft casts hopeful luminosity to light one's way. So it was that Lady Maranda Rockrimmon cast hope upon Faris—set Faris upon a different path—a path of happiness, serenity, and love.

Thus, Faris abandoned the tainted air of Tremeshton in favor of the amethyst sunsets of Loch Loland Castle and her new mistress, Lady Rockrimmon. Further, it was on the very night of her emancipation that Faris first met the man of her dreams—the man of every woman's dreams—the rogue Highwayman of Tanglewood.

Dressed in black and astride his mighty steed, the brave, heroic, and dashing rogue Highwayman of Tanglewood stole Faris's heart as easily as he stole her kiss. Yet the Highwayman of Tanglewood was encircled in mystery—mystery as thick and as secretive as time itself. Could Faris truly own the heart of a man so entirely enveloped in twilight shadows and dangerous secrets?

The Light of the Lovers' Moon
Historical Romance

Violet Fynne was haunted—haunted by memory. It had been nearly ten years since her father had moved the family from the tiny town of Rattler Rock to the city of Albany, New York. Yet the pain and guilt in Violet's heart were as fresh and as haunting as ever they had been.

It was true Violet had been only a child when her family moved. Still—though she had been unwillingly pulled away from Rattler Rock—pulled away from him she held most dear—her heart had never left—and her mind had never forgotten the promise she had made—a promise to a boy—to a boy she had loved—a boy she had vowed to return to.

Yet the world changes—and people move beyond pain and regret. Thus, when Violet Fynne returned to Rattler Rock, it was to find that death had touched those she had known before—that the world had indeed changed—that unfamiliar faces now intruded on beloved memories.

Had she returned too late? Had Violet Fynne lost her chance for peace—and happiness? Would she be forever haunted by the memory of the boy she had loved nearly ten years before?

The Pirate Ruse
Historical Romance

Abducted! Forcibly taken from her home in New Orleans, Cristabel Albay found herself a prisoner aboard an enemy ship—and soon thereafter, transferred into the vile hands of blood-thirsty pirates! War waged between the newly liberated United States and King George. Still, Cristabel would soon discover that British sailors were the very least of her worries—for the pirate captain, Bully Booth, owned no loyalty—no sympathy for those he captured.

Yet hope was not entirely lost—for where there was found one crew of pirates—there was ever found another. Though Cristabel Albay would never have dreamed that she may find fortune in being captured by one pirate captain only to be taken by another—she did! Bully Booth took no man alive—let no woman live long. But the pirate Navarrone was known for his clemency. Thus, Cristabel's hope in knowing her life's continuance was restored.

Nonetheless, as Cristabel's heart began to yearn for the affections of her handsome, beguiling captor—she wondered if Captain Navarrone had only saved her life to execute her poor heart!

The Prairie Prince
Historical Romance

For Katie Matthews, life held no promise of true happiness. Life on the prairie was filled with hard labor, a brutal father, and the knowledge she would need to marry a man incapable of truly loving a woman. Men didn't have time to dote on women—so Katie's father told her. To Katie, it seemed life would forever remain mundane and disappointing—until the day Stover Steele bought her father's south acreage.

Handsome, rugged, and fiercely protective of four orphaned sisters, Stover Steele seemed to have stepped from the pages of some romantic novel. Yet his heroic character and alluring charm only served to remind Katie of what she would never have—true love and happiness the likes found only in fairytales. Furthermore, evil seemed to lurk in the shadows, threatening Katie's brightness, hope, and even her life!

Would Katie Matthews fall prey to disappointment, heartache, and harm? Or could she win the attentions of the handsome Stover Steele long enough to be rescued?

The Rogue Knight
Historical Romance

An aristocratic birthright and the luxurious comforts of profound wealth did nothing to comfort Fontaine Pratina following the death of her beloved parents. After two years in the guardianship of her mother's arrogant and selfish sister, Carileena Wetherton, Fontaine's only moments of joy and peace were found in the company of the loyal servants of Pratina Manor. Only in the kitchens and servants' quarters of her grand domicile did Fontaine find friendship, laughter, and affection.

Always, the life of a wealthy orphan destined to inherit loomed before her—a dark cloud of hopeless, shallow, snobbish people...a life of aristocracy, void of simple joys—and of love. Still, it was her lot—her birthright, and she saw no way of escaping it.

One brutal, cold winter's night a battered stranger appeared at the kitchen servants' entrance, however, seeking shelter and help. He gave only his first name, Knight...and suddenly, Fontaine found herself experiencing fleeting moments of joy in life. For Knight was handsome, powerful...the very stuff of the legends of days of old. Though a servant's class was his, he was proud and strong, and even his name seemed to portray his persona absolutely. He distracted Fontaine from her dull, hopeless existence.

Yet there were devilish secrets—strategies cached

by her greedy aunt, and not even the handsome and powerful Knight could save her from them. Or could he? And if he did—would the truth force Fontaine to forfeit her Knight, her heart's desire…the man she loved—in order to survive?

The Tide of the Mermaid Tears
Historical Romance

Ember Taffee had always lived with her mother and sister in the little cottage by the sea. Her father had once lived there too, but the deep had claimed his life long ago. Still, her existence was a happy one, and Ember found joy, imagination, and respite in the sea and the trinkets it would leave for her on the sand.

Each morning Ember would wander the shore searching for treasures left by the tides. Though she cherished each pretty shell she found, her favorite gifts from Neptune were the rare mermaid tears—bits of tinted glass worn smooth and lovely by the ocean. To Ember, in all the world there were no jewels lovelier than mermaid tears.

Yet one morning, Ember was to discover that Neptune would present her with a gift more rare than any other—something she would value far more than the shells and sea glass she collected. One morning Ember Taffee would find a living, breathing man washed up on the sand—a man who would own claim to her heart as full as Neptune himself owned claim to the seas.

The Time of Aspen Falls
Contemporary Romance

Aspen Falls was happy. Her life was good. Blessed with a wonderful family and a loyal best friend—Aspen did know a measure of contentment.

Still, to Aspen it seemed something was missing—something hovering just beyond her reach—something entirely satisfying that would ensure her happiness. Yet, she couldn't consciously determine what the "something" was. And so, Aspen sailed through life—not quite perfectly content perhaps—but grateful for her measure of contentment.

Grateful, that is, until he appeared—the man in the park—the stranger who jogged passed the bench where Aspen sat during her lunch break each day. As handsome as a dream, and twice as alluring, the man epitomized the absolute stereotypical "real man"—and Aspen's measure of contentment vanished!

Would Aspen Falls reclaim the comfortable contentment she once knew? Or would the handsome real-man-stranger linger in her mind like a sweet, tricky venom—poisoning all hope of Aspen's ever finding true happiness with any other man?

The Touch of Sage
Historical Romance

After the death of her parents, Sage Willows had lovingly nurtured her younger sisters through childhood, seeing each one married and never resenting not finding herself a good man to settle down with. Yet, regret is different than resentment.

Still, Sage found as much joy as a lonely young woman could find, as proprietress of Willows's Boarding House—finding some fulfillment in the companionship of the four beloved widow women boarding with her. But when the devilishly handsome Rebel Lee Mitchell appeared on the boarding house step, Sage's contentment was lost forever.

Dark, mysterious and secretly wounded, Reb Mitchell instantly captured Sage's lonely heart. But the attractive cowboy, admired and coveted by every young unmarried female in his path, seemed unobtainable to Sage Willows. How could a weathered, boarding house proprietress resigned to spinsterhood ever hope to capture the attention of such a man? And without him, would Sage Willows simply sink deeper into bleak loneliness—tormented by the knowledge that the man of every woman's dreams could never be hers?

The Visions of Ransom Lake
Historical Romance

Youthful beauty, naïve innocence, a romantic imagination thirsting for adventure…an apt description of Vaden Valmont, who would soon find the adventure and mystery she had always longed to experience…in the form of a man.

A somber recluse, Ransom Lake descended from his solitary concealment in the mountains, wholly uninterested in people and their trivial affairs. And somehow, young Vaden managed to be ever in his way…either by accident or because of her own unique ability to stumble into a quandary.

Yet the enigmatic Ransom Lake would involuntarily become Vaden's unwitting tutor. Through him, she would experience joy and passion the like even Vaden had never imagined. Yes, Vaden Valmont stepped innocently, yet irrevocably, into love with the secretive, seemingly callous man.

But there were other life's lessons Ransom Lake would inadvertently bring to her as well. The darker side of life—despair, guilt, heartache. Would Ransom Lake be the means of Vaden's dreams come true? Or the cause of her complete desolation?

The Whispered Kiss
Historical Romance

With the sea at its side, the beautiful township of Bostchelan was home to many—including the lovely Coquette de Bellamont, her three sisters, and beloved father. In Bostchelan, Coquette knew happiness and as much contentment as a young woman whose heart had been broken years before could know. Thus, Coquette dwelt in gladness until the day her father returned from his travels with an astonishing tale to tell.

Antoine de Bellamont returned from his travels by way of Roanan bearing a tale of such great adventure to hardly be believed. Further, at the center of Antoine's story loomed a man—the dark Lord of Roanan. Known for his cruel nature, heartlessness, and tendency to violence, the Lord of Roanan had accused Antoine de Bellamont of wrongdoing and demanded recompense. Antoine had promised recompense would be paid—with the hand of his youngest daughter in marriage.

Thus, Coquette found herself lost—thrust onto a dark journey of her own. This journey would find her carried away to Roanan Manor—delivered into the hands of the dark and mysterious Lord of Roanan who dominated it.

The Windswept Flame
Historical Romance

Broken—irreparably broken. The violent deaths of her father and the young man she'd been engaged to marry had irrevocably broken Cedar Dale's heart. Her mother's heart had been broken as well—shattered by the loss of her own true love. Thus, pain and anguish—fear and despair—found Cedar Dale and her mother, Flora, returned to the small western town where life had once been happy and filled with hope. Perhaps there Cedar and her mother would find some resemblance of truly living life—instead of merely existing. And then, a chance meeting with a dream from her past caused a flicker of wonder to ignite in her bosom.

As a child, Cedar Dale had adored the handsome rancher's son, Tom Evans. And when chance brought her face-to-face with the object of her childhood fascination once more, Cedar Dale began to believe that perhaps her fragmented heart could be healed.

Yet could Cedar truly hope to win the regard of

such a man above men as was Tom Evans? A man kept occupied with hard work and ambition—a man so desperately sought after by seemingly every woman?

To Echo the Past
Historical Romance

As her family abandoned the excitement of the city for the uneventful lifestyle of a small, western town, Brynn Clarkston's worst fears were realized. Stripped of her heart's hopes and dreams, Brynn knew true loneliness.

Until an ordinary day revealed a heavenly oasis in the desert...Michael McCall. Handsome and irresistibly charming, Michael McCall (the son of legendary horse breeder Jackson McCall) seemed to offer wild distraction and sincere friendship to Brynn. But could Brynn be content with mere friendship when her dreams of Michael involved so much more?

Weathered Too Young
Historical Romance

Lark Lawrence was alone. In all the world there was no one who cared for her. Still, there were worse things than independence—and Lark had grown quite capable of providing for herself. Nevertheless, as winter loomed, she suddenly found herself with no means by which to afford food and shelter—destitute.

Yet Tom Evans was a kind and compassionate man. When Lark Lawrence appeared on his porch, without pause he hired her to keep house and cook for himself and his cantankerous elder brother, Slater. And although Tom had befriend Lark first, it would be Slater Evans—handsome, brooding, and twelve years Lark's senior—who would unknowingly abduct her heart.

Still, Lark's true age (which she concealed at first meeting the Evans brothers) was not the only truth she had kept from Slater and Tom Evans. Darker secrets lay imprisoned deep within her heart—and her past. However, it is that secrets are made to be found out—and Lark's secrets revealed would soon couple with the arrival of a woman from Slater's past to forever shatter her dreams of winning his love—or so it seemed. Would truth and passion mingle to capture Lark the love she'd never dared to hope for?